a seattle saints novella

pucking all the way

Michelle Hercules

pucking all the way

A Seattle Saints Novella

I've always been the optimistic, glass-half-full kind of girl, and I even have the name to match: Sunshine.

But when I catch my fiancé screwing one of my bridesmaids an hour before our wedding, I can't see the bright side.
Humiliated, I run away and rent a cabin in the woods. I just want to be alone.

But fate has other ideas. It turns out the cabin was double-booked, and now I'm sharing the place with a broody pro hockey player who is as thrilled about my presence as I am about his.

I agree to leave the next morning, but the worst storm in decades hits the mountain, snowing us in.

Trapped, there's nothing to do but make the best of the situation—that is, if Cody Fairchild will let me. He's the most infuriating man I've ever met… and also the sexiest.

Quickly, it becomes clear that there are only two possible outcomes: I'll smother him in his sleep, or I'll screw his brains out. The question is, in what order?

one

. . .

SUNSHINE

I haven't stopped smiling since I put on my wedding dress. It's the most gorgeous garment I've ever seen. Strapless, with a sweetheart neckline and a beaded corset top that makes my boobs look bigger and my waist look tiny. The white silk fabric is smooth with a little sheen. I feel like a princess.

My mother steps behind me in the mirror, her fiery red hair matching mine save for the few strands of gray hair here and there, and rests her chin on my shoulder. "You look beautiful, honey."

I beam. "Thank you."

"Chad won't know what hit him." She winks and then steps away.

The wedding coordinator comes into the wedding party hotel room with frenetic energy and starts issuing orders to the bridesmaids.

"Wait, aren't we missing one?" she asks.

I turn around and count heads—Monica isn't here.

"Yeah, Monica. She stepped away like ten minutes ago," my cousin Phyllis replies, not hiding her contempt.

She's never liked Monica, my best friend from college. Monica was my sorority sister, and we were inseparable during our undergrad years. When I enrolled in vet school and she moved to Miami, we lost the closeness but kept in touch. She was the one who introduced me to Chad in our senior year and naturally had to be part of my wedding party.

"I'll look for her. I bet she's in her room," I say, wanting to check on her privately. Monica's going through a hard time. The guy she's been dating asked to see other people, and she isn't handling the situation well. She thought he was the one. When she told me the story earlier, she broke down, then apologized for being a downer on my wedding day.

"Oh honey, you can't go. You're the bride. What if Chad sees you?" Mom asks.

"Trust me, Mom. Chad won't see me. He's on a different floor. It's no biggie. I'll be back in a flash."

With phone in hand in case I need to text Monica, I hike up my skirt and walk out of the room before anyone can stop me. The wedding coordinator is giving me her trademark disapproving stare, but I've learned to ignore her. She wasn't my first choice to handle my wedding, but my mother is fond of her for whatever reason. Since my parents are paying the bill, I didn't argue.

The hotel hallway is empty, and I sprint toward Monica's room, which is on the same floor as the bride-central room. I'm prepared to knock, but her door isn't shut completely.

I push the door open and walk in... then stop and stare, my heart stuck in my throat. Monica is on her back on the bed with her legs spread wide while Chad is plowing into her.

"What the fuck?" I blurt out.

He stops thrusting and looks at me. His eyes widen, and his face goes ash white. "Sunshine..."

My eyes fill with tears and my pulse thunders in my ears. "I can't believe this."

He jumps off Monica; his dick is still standing at attention. He didn't even use a fucking condom. He takes a step forward, not bothering to hide the evidence of his infidelity, but then why would he? I caught him in the act. "I can explain."

I take a step back, my face hot from the tears rolling down my cheeks. "How long has this been going on?"

His pathetic expression falls, telling me everything I need to know. I look at Monica, who had the decency to cover herself with the bedsheet. "We wanted to tell you but didn't know how."

"It's my fucking wedding day! When exactly were you planning to tell me? On the honeymoon?" The realization hits me then. "Chad's the reason you were crying earlier, isn't he?"

Her guilty look says it all. "Yes. He didn't want to end things with you."

Chad runs a hand through his dark hair. "It's not that I don't love you, Sunshine, but I'm in love with Monica too."

I shake my head. "You're unbelievable. Were you planning to keep us both? Marry me and then keep screwing her on the side?"

When he doesn't answer right away, I know that's *exactly* what he planned to do. Asshole.

"You know what, Chad? I'll make things easy for you. The wedding is off." I turn to Monica. "He's all yours, sweetheart."

Blinded by tears, I run out of the room. I'm not sure where I'm going, but returning to the bridal suite isn't an option. I can't bear the thought of telling everyone what happened. That piece of shit can explain to them why the bride suddenly ran away.

I take the stairs down instead of using the elevator and veer for the nearest exit, trying my best to avoid guests. Outside, the cold Seattle weather hits me in full. It's two days before Christmas, and the ground is covered in snow. But strangely, I'm not bothered by the freezing temperature. I'm running hot, thanks to my anger. Besides not being dressed for the weather, I have a bigger problem. How the hell am I going to get out of here? I left everything in the bridal dressing room, save for my phone.

Then I see the getaway wedding car parked in front of the hotel, decorated with flowers and ribbons and shit, and the words *Just Married* painted in the back window. The key is probably in the vehicle.

I run toward it and get inside before anyone can stop me. Not that I think they would. I'm the bride. They probably think I need something from the car. The key *is* in the ignition, thank God. I start the car and peel out of the parking spot, burning rubber. I have no idea where I'm going, but anywhere is better than here.

After ten minutes, my mom calls me. I don't answer. Then my dad and Phyllis call, and I let those go to voice mail too. More texts and calls come but I don't even look at my phone anymore to know which one of my friends is trying to reach me. I wonder if Chad already told them the news. I feel bad about ignoring them, but I need to sort out my thoughts before I talk to them. They'll probably beg me to return to the hotel, and that's the last thing I want to do. It is getting late though, and I can't drive forever.

I stop at a gas station, then look at the Airbnb app. I want a place to lie low for a few days, something secluded. I need to hide away from the world and think about everything. I had my entire life planned out. Become a veterinarian and join my dad's practice, marry Chad, have kids. Besides my career, which I love, the rest is now a big black void. I don't know if I'll be able to trust another man after Chad's betrayal with someone I considered a friend.

After inserting a few keywords in the app's search bar, the perfect rental pops up. It's a cabin in the woods, an hour from Seattle and far from civilization. And it's available this weekend, which is surprising. If that's not a sign that I'm making the right decision, I don't know what is. Isolation, here I come. God, I sound like Elsa from *Frozen*. I'm already wearing the big princess dress. Now I just need to belt out the lyrics to "Let it Go."

Easier said than done, Elsa. But I will get through.

two

· · ·

CODY

It's been a week since I was benched, thanks to an upper-body injury caused by sheer bad luck. I tripped over the opposing team's goalie's stick and collided hard with the boards. My arm is now in a sling, and the Saints athletic staff told me I need another week of rest before I can resume training. It isn't ideal, but it's also not the end of the world. Though it'd be more bearable if Penelope weren't trying to use my injury to weasel her way back into my life.

I dated her for three months, and we've been broken up for two. In the beginning, it was fun. She was a model, hot and open to experimenting in the bedroom. But then she began dropping hints about engagement rings and weddings left and right. When I ignored those, she stopped being fun in the sack, which made me suspect she wasn't as into it as I'd thought. She was only going along with me in the hopes that I would fall for her and marry her.

If she had done her homework, she would've known that marriage is not something I'll ever consider. I've been extremely vocal about it in interviews when people ask about my dating status. Not that it happens often, thank fuck. Most reporters stick to hockey.

I don't believe in marriage. My parents have an awful one. They should have divorced a long time ago, but they stuck with it, and I don't know why. They fought most of the time while I was growing up. They probably still do, but I don't speak to them anymore. I want distance from their toxicity.

I need to get the hell out of this town before Penelope tracks me down. She's been texting and calling constantly and even sent me a basket filled with my favorite snacks. I suspect her next move will be to show up at my place out of the blue. She wouldn't be able to come up, thanks to the security in my building in Pike Place, but I want to save us both the headache nonetheless.

It's past eight, and the city lights are twinkling in the distance. I live on the top floor of a fifteen-story building, and the panoramic view from my living room is spectacular. The sky is clear tonight, but snow still covers the sidewalk and trees below.

I call my older sister Gigi, hoping I can stay in the cabin she has listed on Airbnb. I can get there in an hour. It's rustic and small, with only one bedroom, but it has a hot tub, and the bonus is that it's in the middle of the woods, far from civilization. I hope it's not rented.

She answers on the second ring. "Hey Cody, what's up?"

"Not much."

"Have you changed your mind about spending Christmas with us now that you're benched?"

My excuse for never flying to San Diego to spend Christmas with her has always been hockey. They moved to Cali five years ago when Jon, my brother-in-law, got offered a job there. More often than not, we play during the holidays, so I'm not surprised she assumes I planned to make the trip south this year. Yes, the weather is nicer in California, but unlike most people, I actually do like winter.

"No, I don't think so. I need peace and quiet and I won't get that by hanging out with you and your litter."

"Are you calling my kids animals?" She fakes indignation.

"You know what they are—little hellions. Would it kill you and your husband to teach them some manners?" I tease.

While I have an aversion to marriage, Gigi married

right after college and got busy popping out kids. She has four—two boys, two girls, and another girl on the way. The oldest is six and the youngest is two. I love my nephews and nieces, but right now, I really shouldn't be around little kids who will want to play and horse around. It's a bad idea with my injury, and there's also the fact I hate Christmas.

"You suck," she replies. "If you're not calling to tell me you're coming for Christmas, what do you want?"

"I was wondering if I could stay at your cabin for a few days."

"The cabin you said was a stupid idea to buy?" I can almost see her brows rise.

"Yes, Gigi. That cabin."

"Sure, but under one condition."

I sigh. "Sure, what is it?"

"You need to come here for the birth of your niece."

"Gigi... come on. You're about to pop, and I'm in the middle of a hockey season."

"I don't care. Players leave all the time to be with their wives for the birth of their children."

"You said the magic word. They leave to be with their *wives*. You're my sister, and you have a husband."

"Fine. But the moment you have a break, you have to come visit. Do not wait until her first birthday like you did with the others."

"All right, you have a deal." I head to my bedroom

so I can pack quickly. I want to arrive at the cabin before ten. "Is the code for the cabin still the same?"

"Yep. Have fun alone at Christmas, Mr. Scrooge."

"Don't worry, sis. I will. I'm looking forward to being blissfully alone."

three

. . .

SUNSHINE

Before I take the winding road up to the cabin—at least, I imagine the road will be twisty—I stop at a small convenience store to buy supplies. I don't expect the cabin to have any food or even wood if there's a fireplace. I want to be alone, but I don't want to die of starvation or freeze to death.

The looks I receive as I enter the store are mortifying. Quizzical eyebrows and jaws hanging loose, but nobody asks me why I'm wearing a strapless wedding dress and no coat when it's freezing outside.

I don't want to spend longer than necessary here under the watchful eyes, so I turn and ask a teenager who's stocking shelves where I can find everything I need.

He points me in several different directions. Perhaps I should have asked him one thing. I take a cart and start filling it with comfort food. Bread, cakes, chocolate, cookies, and definitely ice cream, but I also load up on nutritious items—or as nutritious as I can get in such a store. Eggs, milk, peanut butter, apples, bananas, and a few frozen meals.

I booked the cabin through the weekend, so that means I'll spend Christmas alone. The thought is depressing, but I'll be miserable no matter where I am. My parents will be disappointed, but I need time to be by myself. I hope they understand.

I see that they sell booze here too, and I make a beeline for that aisle. I'm not a big drinker, and I usually stick to wine, but I have a feeling the offerings here are more likely to give me a headache than a buzz. I decide to buy bottles of whiskey and gin. They also sell eggnog, so I grab that too. I can be miserable *and* in the Christmas spirit at the same time.

The last item on the list is the firewood. There are only two bags left, and I buy both, hoping it will be enough. The cashier keeps staring at me as she rings up my items, but she doesn't ask why I'm wearing a wedding dress. I wonder if my makeup is completely ruined, thanks to the tears. The makeup artists used waterproof mascara, banking on the fact that I'd cry at the ceremony. What a joke.

"I'll need to see ID," the cashier tells me, waking me from my reverie.

Shit. I don't have my purse on me. I can pay using my phone, but I forgot they'd ask to see my driver's license because of the booze.

"I don't have one on me. I left in a hurry."

She arches her brows. "I was wondering about that. I'm sorry, hon. I can't sell you alcohol without seeing an ID."

I remember that I had to take a picture of my license the other day, so I ask, "Would a photo of it be enough?"

"I don't know…"

"Please. Don't ask me to spend Christmas alone without booze after I caught my fiancé screwing one of my bridesmaids an hour before our wedding."

She widens her eyes. "Oh my. That's terrible. Oh, I shouldn't really do this, but what the hell."

I show her the picture on my phone, and she nods, satisfied.

"Thank you so much." I put all the bags in the cart, then wish her a Merry Christmas before wheeling my trove out of the store.

Shivers run down my spine, and my teeth start to chatter. Now that the adrenaline has left my body, I can feel the full blast of the cold. It doesn't help that it was nice and toasty inside the store, and my body is rebelling against the drastic change in temperature. Too bad they don't sell any clothing. I'd kill for a sweatshirt.

As if reading my mind, the cashier runs out of the store and drapes something warm over my shoulders.

"What is this?" I ask, touching the soft fabric.

"It's a poncho I knitted. I'm guessing you don't have any winter clothes in your car, do you?"

"No. I only have this." I gesture at my dress.

"There are a few clothing stores down the road. They're closed now, but they'll be open tomorrow at nine."

"Thank you so much for the poncho. How much do you want for it?"

She widens her eyes and shakes her head. "Don't be silly, hon. It's a gift."

My eyes fill with tears. Kindness from strangers hits differently. "Thank you. This means a lot."

"You're welcome, dear. You take care, all right? And Merry Christmas."

She returns to the store, and I quickly put all my groceries in the trunk, trying to ignore the *Just Married* text painted on the window. The first thing I'll do tomorrow morning is scrape the paint off. I don't need another reminder that I was supposed to be a married woman by now, celebrating with the man I thought was the love of my life. How could I have been so stupid?

I hastily wipe away the tears rolling down my cheeks before they freeze, then get behind the steering wheel. I turn on the engine, and while I wait for the car to get warm, I put on my new poncho. I've never treasured a piece of clothing more.

The navigation system tells me I'm fifteen minutes away from the cabin. As I put the car in drive, my mother calls again. Now that I'm far enough from the city—and calmer—I accept the call.

"Hi Mom."

"Sunshine. Oh my God, darling. We've been worried sick. Where are you?"

I definitely don't want to tell my parents my location because I know they'll come and try to drag me back to their house.

"It doesn't matter where I am. I'm fine. I just need some time alone."

"Oh no, honey. That's the last thing you need. After such betrayal, you need to be surrounded by the people who love you."

My stomach ties into knots. "So Chad told you what he did?"

Mom snorts. "No. Phyllis went looking for you and found him with Monica. Your father had to be restrained because he was going to kick the shit out of that scumbag."

Oh, Dad.

"I'm so sorry, Mom."

"Honey, you have nothing to be sorry about. The

only people in the wrong here are Chad and that Monicunt."

Monicunt.

Crazy laughter bubbles up. "Who came up with that?"

"Phyllis. But it caught on pretty quickly."

It tracks. And my cousin was right about Monica. She wasn't my friend.

"The name fits her too," Mom continues. "I mean, what was she wearing at the rehearsal dinner? A short, tight dress that was two sizes too small for her and made her look like a sausage about to burst. We all thought she looked like a crack whore."

"Mom!"

My mother was never one to mince words. She thinks she's helping me by trashing Monica, but she's only making it worse. She isn't wrong in her assessment, but despite all that, Chad was more than happy to fuck her minutes before getting married to me. I think he deserves more bashing than Monica.

"We tried to come up with a name for Chad too, but nothing stuck. We'll keep working on it," Mom says.

"I don't want to talk about them. I just want to forget everything."

Specifically, I want to erase that disgusting image of them fucking from my mind. The memory alone brings bile to my mouth. I need to get tested too. I don't believe Chad was only screwing Monica. Once a cheater, always a cheater. God, I don't want to think about it now. I might have to pull over and vomit.

The navigation system gives me new directions, and Mom overhears it. "What was that? Are you still on the road?"

"Yes, Mom. I'm almost at my destination. I'll call you later, okay?"

"Honey, are you sure you don't want to come home?"

Home. My parents' house in Laurelhurst hasn't been home to me since I went to Washington State University. But I guess, to my parents, their house will always be my home.

"I'll come after Christmas, okay? I promise."

"All right. We'll wait for you to celebrate."

"No, Mom. Don't cancel your plans because of me. Please."

She sniffs. "This is all so very terrible, hon. The entire family is in shock. No one is in a festive mood now."

Guilt pierces my chest. I hate that my personal drama is ruining my mother's favorite holiday.

"You can see what happened as a blessing. I dodged a bullet."

"I suppose you're right. We'll celebrate that then, but you should too."

"I'll get there. I'll call later, Mom."

"All right, honey. We love you."

"I love you too."

I'm in tears again after the call, and to cheer myself up, I find a station that plays Christmas songs. When Wham!'s "Last Christmas" pours out of the speakers, I take it as a sign that my true love is still out there. Chad was a detour. As sad as I am right now, I belt out the lyrics as loud as I can. My heart is bleeding, but it will mend... eventually.

four

SUNSHINE

Mercifully, I don't get lost on the way to the cabin. It's super secluded, and in the darkness, the forest is a bit spooky. I never realized I was leery of nature until I had to walk from the car to the cabin. It irks me that I can't see anything beyond the halo from the headlights. Anyone or anything could be watching me.

Stop being silly, Sunshine. There's nothing out there.

Not true; there are bears, and I have food in the car. Argh.

No, they should be hibernating now.

There are steps leading up to the front door and no illumination whatsoever in front of the tiny building, hence why I left my headlights on.

The steps are covered in snow, and my bejeweled wedding shoes sink into it. They're satin-covered and most likely will be ruined, but walking barefoot in the snow is not something I'm willing to do. I hold up my long skirt with one hand and grip the wood railing with the other. Slipping and breaking my neck in the middle of nowhere is not how I want my story to end.

The cabin is rustic, but the lock on the door is ultra-modern. It's a pad with a code. I already have the email with the instructions open, so I glance at the screen and type the code quickly. The soft sound that comes from the pad reminds me of a spell cast by a Disney character. I push the door open and immediately turn on the lights.

This isn't a log cabin, but it is made of light wood, and I'm hit with the fresh, earthy scent of cedar, citrus, and a hint of campfire. A small open kitchen is on the far wall with a counter that separates it from the living room. To my right, there's a breakfast nook that fits exactly four people. A two-seater couch faces the fire-place, but there's no coffee table in front of it, just a big fake fur rug that looks soft and inviting.

My eyes zero in on the thick blanket draped over the couch. I wrap it around my shoulders over the poncho before I venture out to get the groceries from the car. It takes me two trips to get everything inside. I make sure the door is properly locked before I put the groceries away.

As I predicted, it's freezing inside. I didn't expect the cabin to have central heating. But I'm glad to see several bags of firewood next to the fireplace. Combined with what I got, it should be enough to last through the weekend.

I inspect the only bedroom in the cabin. It has a queen-size bed with a thick duvet and fluffy pillows. There's a portable electric heater inside. Thank fuck. The bedroom isn't a suite because there's only one bathroom in the cabin, which is big enough to fit a small sink, a toilet, and a shower. I didn't read the description of the place in detail, but it did say four people can sleep here. I'm assuming the couch is a pullout.

I can't imagine sharing the space with three other people. I'd probably develop claustrophobia.

I debate what to do next—start a fire or get some alcohol in me. Whiskey will warm me up quicker. I take a couple of shots, then try to take my dress off. Fuck. I can't reach the laces to slacken them. I guess it's staying on for now.

It's too quiet in the cabin, and I look around for a sound system. I don't want to use my phone to listen to music—I need to preserve the battery since I don't have a charger with me. Thankfully, I find an old radio in one of the kitchen cabinets. I put it on and try to find the Christmas music station again.

Mariah is playing now, and even though it isn't exactly the song I want to listen to, I don't change the station. Instead, I take another shot of whiskey and work on the fireplace. After a few failed attempts, flames soar to life.

"Yes!" I raise one fist in the air while holding the bottle of whiskey with the other.

I should probably eat something, but I'm suddenly too tired to bother. I turn off the lights and collapse in a heap in front of the fire, cradling the whiskey bottle against my chest while singing Christmas songs until my eyelids turn heavy. I lie on the soft rug and watch the flames dance until everything goes dark.

I wake up to the sound of wind chimes, or is it Tinkerbell casting a spell? I open my eyes, confused as hell. Ugh. I drank too much whiskey. The bottle is still nestled against my chest, and it's pitch black in the room. The fire died some time ago, so there's no heat coming from the fireplace anymore.

Then the front door opens, and adrenaline spikes in my veins. I have an intruder.

I jump to my feet at the same time that someone turns on the light. I don't stop to think before I toss the bottle of whiskey at the man, missing his head by an inch.

"What the fuck!" he yells, then narrows his eyes dangerously.

Damn everything to hell. I'm so screwed.

24

five

. . .

CODY

It takes me longer than planned to get to the cabin, mainly because I stopped to buy groceries and the shop I prefer wasn't on the way. When I was halfway to the cabin, it started to snow heavily, which slowed my drive. That was the first surprise of the evening. The weather forecast didn't include snowfall.

The second surprise is the car parked in front of the cabin, decorated with white flowers and ribbons with the phrase *Just Married* painted on the back window.

Immediately, I suspect that Penelope found out I was coming here, and this is her psycho way of telling me she won't let go. Irritated, I get out of my truck and look inside the car. There's no one in it. I also check the perimeter of the cabin and see no signs of her. She couldn't get inside unless she had the lock code, and my sister would never give that information to Penelope. She was relieved when I ended things with her.

Nonetheless, I'm wary when I open the front door, and that's the only reason I manage to avoid getting hit by a flying whiskey bottle tossed by a redheaded woman in a wedding dress.

"What the fuck!" I yell, narrowing my eyes.

I'm pissed. I could have gotten seriously hurt. But my aggravation wilts a fraction when I see her frightened gaze locked on my face. Her chest is rising and falling fast, thanks to her erratic breathing.

She reaches for the fire poker and holds it with both hands. "Stay away from me!"

Damn everything to hell. The last thing I had in mind when I asked to use Gigi's cabin was to deal with a deranged stranger hell-bent on killing me. I lift my right palm since my left arm is in a sling. "Calm down. I'm not going to hurt you."

"That's exactly what a serial killer would say before he chopped me to bits."

"I'm not a serial killer," I grit out, trying my best to rein in my temper. "My name is Cody Fairchild. I play for the Seattle Saints. The NHL team," I add, in case she doesn't follow hockey.

"So you say. Besides, being a pro hockey player doesn't mean you don't like to play Dexter on the side."

I'd laugh if it weren't for this fucked-up situation. This had better not be a prank set up by my teammate Nate. We're cousins, and he could have planned this whole thing with Gigi's help.

"This is probably just a misunderstanding," I say, reaching for the phone in my pocket. "Let me call my si—"

"Stop right there." She pulls her arm back, keeping the fire poker aimed at me. "Keep your hand where I can see it, or I'll shish kebab you."

I widen my eyes, taking her seriously. She looks unhinged with that wedding dress topped by the ugliest poncho I've ever seen. Whoever knitted that decided to use all colors available. This woman is either an excellent actress, or she's truly fucking terrified of me. As annoyed as I am, I need to tread carefully. I'd rather be the butt of a joke than set this woman off. Scared people will do the craziest shit.

"I was only going to call my sister. She owns this cabin. She told me it was free this weekend."

The woman blinks fast, then lowers her arm. "Okay. Call her then."

Slowly, I take my phone out and call Gigi, putting it on speaker.

"Cody, twice in a day. You'd better be calling now to

say you've changed your mind about coming to San Diego."

"No, that's not it. You're on speaker, by the way. I'm at your cabin and found out it was already occupied."

"What do you mean it's occupied?"

"There's a woman here, wearing a wedding dress and ready to skewer me with the fire poker."

"What?" Gigi shrieks.

"She isn't an early Christmas gift for me, is she?" I joke but realize immediately it was a mistake.

"I'm not a gift, you perv!" Bride from Hell brandishes her makeshift weapon.

"Oh my God, Cody! How could you say something like that?"

"Sorry. Just be straight with me, all right? This isn't a prank you set up with Nate, is it?"

"Of course not. How can you ask that?"

"Because you and Nate love pulling shit like this." I keep my eyes on my companion, lest she decide to use the fire poker on me after all.

"I swear it, Cody. It isn't a prank. Hold on, let me check my email."

While I wait for my sister, I ask the woman, "Are you convinced now that I'm not a serial killer?"

"No." She keeps glaring at me with her bright-blue eyes.

"Okay, I'm back," Gigi says. "I fucked up. The cabin

was booked minutes after I said it was free. With my pregnancy brain, I forgot to mark it as unavailable. I'm so sorry, Sunshine."

I snort. "Sunshine? You don't need to call me pretty names, sis."

"She isn't talking to you," the woman replies. *"I'm* Sunshine."

My brows shoot to the heavens. "Your name is *Sunshine?"*

"Yes," she hisses. "Sunshine Winters. Why? Do you have a problem with that?"

Jesus. Sunshine Winters. What a stupid name. But I don't have a death wish, so I shake my head. "Nope, not at all."

"This is a disaster," Gigi whines, reminding me that I'm still on the call with her. "You have to leave, Cody."

Hell to the fucking no. I didn't come all the way here to simply turn around. I look outside and all I can see are the flurries of snow that are thicker now. "Can't. It isn't safe. It's snowing heavily now, and with my arm, I don't want to risk the drive."

"I can't go either," Sunshine replies. "I've been drinking." Her gaze switches to what's left of the whiskey bottle. Shards of glass are spread everywhere.

"I guess you'll have to share the cabin for one night, then," Gigi replies. "I'm so sorry, Sunshine. I swear you're safe with my brother. He might make inappropriate jokes and hate Christmas, but he's harmless. I'll refund your money."

Sunshine's face falls. I'm sure she was expecting me to hit the road. Besides the fact I really don't want to drive back tonight, I wasn't kidding about it not being safe.

"All right, sis. I'd better get settled. I'll call you tomorrow."

I end the call, and immediately Gigi texts me.

> Cody, please behave.

> > What do you think I'm gonna do?

> Be your aggro self.

> > As long as Sunshine doesn't get in my way, it'll be fine.

> It's a tiny cabin. Of course she'll get in the way!

Fuck. Sharing a small space with a stranger is the last thing I want to do. I don't even bother replying to Gigi.

"I'd better clean up that mess." Sunshine sets the fire poker down and walks to the kitchen. "Do you know where the broom is?"

"No," I grumble.

She starts opening cabinets until she finds what she's looking for. When she faces me, I notice how gorgeous she is. Now that she isn't threatening to kill me, I can appreciate her looks. Long red hair that cascades in soft curls down her back, high cheekbones and full, bee-stung lips. Shit. She's the type of woman I'd go for. But I'm still annoyed as hell, and it'll take a while for the aggravation to leave my system.

She doesn't make eye contact with me when she returns to the living room. On impulse, I touch her arm. She jumps back, her eyes turning rounder. I don't think the phone call with Gigi put her at ease.

I clear my throat. "I'm sorry I scared you. Are you okay?"

Her eyes widen, and I notice they're bloodshot. Has she been crying? Her makeup isn't smudged though.

"I'm not okay, but don't worry, you're not the cause. You can take the bedroom. I'll sleep on the couch, and tomorrow, I'll get out of your hair."

I was planning to sleep in the bedroom, but instead, I find myself saying, "I can sleep on the couch. You got here first."

Maybe her comment about not being okay softened me a little. I'm curious why she isn't, and that wedding dress probably means she went through something major, but I won't ask. Prying isn't my thing. Besides, she might decide to use me as her shrink, and giving advice to people—especially strangers—is not what I do best. I'm brutally honest, and that's never what people want.

She shakes her head and glances at the dark fireplace. "I fell asleep on the rug earlier. The couch is an upgrade." She returns her attention to me. "Besides, I don't think you'd fit on the couch."

For some idiotic reason, I feel smug about her comment. I grin. "It's a pullout."

"I know. But in any case, if you restart the fire while I clean up the mess, that'd be great."

"I can do that. Let me get my stuff out of my truck first."

I stride out of the cabin before Sunshine turns me into a soft idiot. I want to hold on to my irritation for as long as I can so I don't think about the real reason I'm annoyed. I hate that I'm benched. Pure and simple. I miss the ice, the physical exertion, the adrenaline, and the fights.

The weather has taken a turn for the worse. At this rate, it'll be a pain in the ass to drive back to civilization. I glance at Sunshine's car. It's a sedan and probably doesn't have four-wheel drive. It could be dangerous to drive that thing, even during the day.

Hell, I can't ask her to leave tomorrow. I should go. My truck can handle rough terrain better. But what if the weather worsens and she gets stuck here? I rub my face. Fuck. I won't think about it now.

With the use of only one arm, I have to make two trips to unload everything. When I return the second time with the groceries, Sunshine has finished cleaning, and she's now standing in front of the open fridge.

She looks over her shoulder and asks. "I'm going to cook dinner. Are you hungry?"

I'm not that hungry. I ate a sandwich before I left the house, but I find myself saying. "Yes, I'm starving."

And I know I'm not talking about food.

six

· · ·

SUNSHINE

Cody's presence in the cabin was explained, but I'm still shaking from head to toe. I'm reeling from the sheer panic I felt when I thought someone had broken in to harm me. It was the most stressful and awful experience of my life. It even beat finding Chad fucking Monica. It also puts things in perspective. I have little energy left in me now to care about those two backstabbers.

I don't want Cody to notice I'm still rattled—it wasn't his fault that his sister messed up the booking system. I wonder why his arm is in a sling. He said he's a hockey player, so maybe he got hurt during a game. I hope nothing serious. I veer for the kitchen to cook something and distract myself. I haven't eaten all day. I need to put food in my belly, especially after all the whiskey I drank. I'm already developing a headache. I should drink some water too.

Cody comes in carrying a large duffel bag and puts that in the bedroom, then goes out again. When he returns and closes the door, I look over my shoulder and ask if he's hungry. The way he tells me he's starving does something to my insides. I don't know if it's his tone or the smoldering way he's looking at me with those intense green eyes that make my heart beat a little faster.

"They didn't have a lot of variety at the grocery store," I say. "I can make us scrambled eggs and toast."

"I brought food." He lifts two full grocery bags with one arm, emphasizing the biceps under his coat.

I shouldn't be surprised he's in top shape, considering what he does for a living. I begin to wonder what he looks like without all those clothes.

"Is there something wrong?" he asks.

Oops. I was ogling him. I shake my head. "No."

He smirks. Damn it. He caught me checking him out. My face heats in an instant, and I know I'm blushing. I turn away and look inside the fridge, hoping the cold blast will bring my face's coloring back to normal.

I tense the moment I sense his presence right behind me.

"Can I get to the fridge?"

"Yeah, sure." I step aside to give him access, but thanks to the minuscule size of the kitchen, we're now super close. To get out of the way completely, I need to slide past him, and my puffy skirt doesn't help.

I decide to stay put and not move from my corner. "What do you have?"

"Steaks, pork, sausage, ham, a variety of cheeses, potatoes, salad, some fruit… and another bottle of whiskey, if you're interested." He looks at me, and there isn't a hint of a smile on his face.

I get defensive in an instant. "I'm not a drunk."

His brows arch. "I didn't say you were. But you were sleeping next to a bottle of whiskey, weren't you?"

My face turns into lava. "So? I was having a bad day. A person is allowed to drown their sorrows in booze."

"Does your bad day have anything to do with what you're wearing?"

Damn it. I don't want to talk about my disastrous evening. I came here to forget about it. I take a step back. "It's none of your business."

He closes the fridge door and stands to his full height. He's a good head taller than me, so I need to crane my neck to keep staring at his face. "Listen, Sunshine. I'm trying to be civil. You're wearing a wedding dress under the ugliest poncho I've ever seen. Not the typical attire for a cabin in the woods. Forgive my curiosity."

I cross my arms. "If that's you being civil, your report card would say try harder."

He narrows his eyes. "I get it. This is a shitty situation. I want to be here with you as much as you want to be with me. Let's try to survive the night."

"Fine. Do you still want dinner?"

"No, not really."

Disappointment floods me, and I don't know why. "I thought you were starving."

"I lost my appetite." He takes a bottle of red wine from his grocery bag and heads for the bedroom.

"Where are you going?" My heart seems to shrivel inside my chest. He's rude as fuck, but his company is distracting.

"To sleep."

"I thought you were going to start the fire for me."

He turns to me, then switches his attention to the fireplace. "Did you start a fire before you fell asleep?"

"Yes."

He nods. "Then you can do it again."

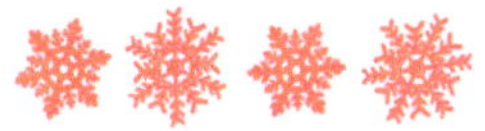

cody

What the fuck did I just do? I had every intention of controlling my temper and not taking my frustration out on Sunshine, but I did exactly that at the first opportunity. Would it kill me to start the fire for her?

I sit on the edge of the bed and set the bottle of wine on the nightstand. It's a very expensive wine that I'd planned to sip in front of the fireplace. Drinking it out of the bottle in my bed is a waste. I rub my face and think about my next move.

Get back out there and apologize to the girl, you idiot.

My phone pings, distracting me. I glance at the screen. I set up notifications to update me on game scores. We're losing to the Titans already. They scored thirty seconds after puck drop. Fuck me. The rivalry between our teams is one of the biggest in the NHL. I'm leading in the number of points scored, and my absence from the game will be felt.

I remember service being terrible up here, and tonight reveals it hasn't improved. I can't watch the game live on my phone. Annoyed, I toss the phone on the mattress. One of the reasons I came to the cabin was to not obsess about tonight's game. And here I am, doing just that. I have to trust that the head coach, Markus, will use the right players to compensate for my absence.

Nate must be pissed though. He's our enforcer and usually on the starting lineup. And considering Ryan Bertrand—the cockiest motherfucker I've ever met—scored the first goal, there will be blood.

Sunshine's scream makes me jump from the bed and

run back into the living room. My heart leaps to my throat. Her big skirt is on fire and she's trying to put it out by beating the flames with her hand. I grab the blanket from the couch and cover the flames with it. It isn't a big fire, and it goes out immediately.

I look up from my crouched position, breathing hard. Adrenaline is coursing through my veins, and my pulse is beating in my ears. "Are you okay?"

She steps away from me and collapses to the floor in a heap, her shoulders slouching forward. "No, I'm not okay." Her voice is tight, as if she's on the verge of tears.

"Did you get burned? Let me see your legs."

"I'm not burned. I'm just fucking pathetic." Her entire body begins to shake as she breaks down in front of me. Fat tears run down her cheeks, and her sobs are loud and ugly.

I'm at a loss. Sunshine is breaking in front of me, and I don't know what to do. There's a strange heaviness in my chest though. "You aren't pathetic."

"Yes, I am." She wipes her wet cheeks with the back of her forearm. The action makes her look like a young, freckled kid. It's kind of adorable. "I can't even start a damn fire without burning myself to a crisp."

"Let's face it, that isn't the best attire for starting fires," I tease, hoping it'll lighten the mood. Her scowl tells me I missed the mark again.

"I have nothing else to wear."

"Thank fuck."

Her brows shoot to the heavens. "What?"

"Not having anything else to wear is definitely better than choosing to stay in a wedding dress."

She chuckles and sniffs. "Has anyone ever told you that you suck at making people feel better?"

I cock an eyebrow. "Do I, though? You were crying a second ago, and now you're laughing."

Her expression shuts down again, and her forehead wrinkles. "I'm not laughing."

I unfurl from my crouch and offer her my hand. "Come on. Let's get you off the floor and out of that dress."

Her pretty eyes widen, and her luscious lips form a perfect *O*. Jesus, why am I noticing all those details about her appearance? Is "damsel in distress" my thing now?

She doesn't take my hand. "Out of this dress and into what?"

I press my lips together. Why is she being so difficult? Before I say something rude, I turn around and head to my room. Damn infuriating woman.

seven

SUNSHINE

I watch Cody disappear into the bedroom in disbelief. Is he serious? What did I say that pissed him off this time? I *just* told him I had nothing else to wear, and he wanted me to get out of my dress. My question was valid. I get up from my sprawled position on the floor and inspect the damage to my dress. I had no intention of wearing this damn thing again, but it's a shame it got destroyed. I could have donated it.

A moment later, Cody returns to the living room carrying a stack of folded clothes. "Here. You can wear some of mine."

I stare at his offering for a second too long before looking at his face. "You want me to wear your clothes?"

"No. I brought these out and told you to wear them just for kicks. In reality, I'd rather you wear nothing at all."

My pulse accelerates. His face is serious; there isn't a hint of mirth in his eyes. I can't tell if he's pissed or if he really wants to see me naked. He's impossible to read.

"Was that another one of your stupid jokes?"

"Do you see me laughing?"

Now my stomach gets all twisted and my eyes bug out. Is Cody flirting with me? I've never met a guy whose game could be confused with *I want to murder you*. I don't know how to respond, so I just stare at his maddening, sinfully hot face. His forest-green eyes are intense and alluring. They're like hook, line, and sinker, and my stupid self is screaming, *Reel me in, reel me in*.

No good can come of entertaining the idea of sleeping with him. His attitude spells trouble with a capital *T*.

"You're not going to run to the hills, are you?" he asks when I don't reply right away.

"No, I'm not going to run away again. I like to space out my escapes to once a week."

His lips curl upward. It's not a grin, but it's probably the best I'll get from him. "Do you want the clothes or not?"

I take the stack from him. "Yes. Thank you. But uh… don't take this the wrong way, but I'll need help getting my corset unlaced."

He arches a brow. "I'm curious... what exactly would be the *wrong* way to take your request?"

Heat creeps up my cheeks. Oh how I hate the way my body betrays me. "I don't want you getting any ideas."

He steps closer, invading my space. "What ideas shouldn't I be getting, Sunshine?"

Hummingbirds seem to be trapped inside my rib cage, and my breathing becomes shallow. I flatten my palm against his broad chest and push him back. "Stop this nonsense. I know you're just messing with me."

He stares without saying a word for a couple beats, unnerving me. I don't know if he's teasing or not, but it's better if he thinks I believe that's what's going on here.

"All right. I won't get any ideas. Now turn around."

Ugh. Why does he have to sound so bossy? And why does it make me tingle all over? I offer my back to him before I run my mouth again. When he doesn't say anything, I look over my shoulder and find him staring at the corset as if he's trying to solve a math equation. "What?"

"How long did it take to get you all laced up like that?"

"Not as long as you'd think."

"Jesus, I don't know where to start. Can I cut the laces with scissors?"

"No!"

My outburst makes him glance up. "Do you plan on wearing a half-burned dress again?"

"It's the only piece of clothing I have to my name besides the poncho. I'd rather not ruin it completely."

"What? Do you think I'm going to demand that you return my clothes tomorrow before you drive home?"

"Aren't you?"

"They're sweats, Sunshine. You can keep them. I have hundreds more at home."

"Hundreds? How many sweats does a guy need?"

He narrows his eyes. "Do you want this thing off or not?"

"Yeah," I mumble, facing the fireplace again.

Cody starts to work on the laces, and it feels intimate. When his fingers brush my skin, rivulets of desire run down my spine, shocking me. The whole point of the laces was to make Chad work for it. Now I have this annoyingly gorgeous man doing the job, and even though we're strangers, and he's as prickly as a cactus, my pulse is beating furiously fast. What the hell is wrong with me? I can't even blame my feelings on alcohol because I'm definitely not drunk anymore.

I close my eyes and pretend I'm not a cheated-on bride whose life is a mess. Would it be so bad if I let my body make the decisions for a change? Running away in my wedding dress was the most impulsive thing I've ever done in my life, and it was the right thing to do.

Maybe sleeping with Cody would also be the right thing to do.

The corset slackens, and Cody says, "There. It's done."

I hold the front—so I don't flash him—and turn around. He doesn't step back, and we're once again in each other's space. My breath catches as our eyes lock. Neither of us speaks, and the atmosphere seems to crackle with electricity.

"Thank you," I croak.

"You can use the bedroom to change," he says in a voice that's a little tight, a little rough.

"Okay." I hurry into the bedroom before I succumb to the charged moment we shared.

Now I'm sure Cody wasn't joking. He wants me, and I don't know what to do with the knowledge.

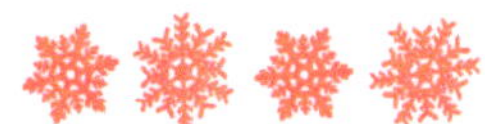

cody

I'm still looking toward the bedroom, even though Sunshine disappeared inside. I don't know how I let things get out of hand like that. I made no attempt to hide I was attracted to her. I was a second away from kissing her, but then my sanity returned. Hooking up with Sunshine isn't a smart idea. I don't know why she ran away from her own wedding with nothing but the clothes on her back, but that alone is reason enough to stay the hell away from her. Vulnerable women make terrible hookups. They have the tendency to develop romantic feelings faster. I came here to hide from a clingy ex. I don't need another headache, even if said headache is a feisty, infuriating, sexy redhead with a mouth that begs to be kissed.

Forget the wine. I need something stronger. I take the bottle of whiskey I bought and fill a glass halfway, not bothering with ice. Then I shoot it back, welcoming the heat that goes down my throat smoothly. I have time for one more shot before she walks out of the bedroom wearing my clothes.

I go utterly still and drink her in. Naturally, my sweats are huge on her, making her seem smaller than she is. I can barely see the swell of her breasts anymore, but I know they're there. I imagine what they look like, and my cock stirs in my pants. Perhaps drinking those shots of whiskey wasn't the smartest idea.

"How do I look?" She places a hand on her hip and lifts her other arm, striking a pose.

"Like you drank a shrinking potion," I lie, trying to hide what she's doing to me.

She makes a face, lowering her arm. "Boy, you are a grump, aren't you?"

"I've been called worse."

She notices the whiskey bottle on the counter, and asks, "Changed your mind about the wine?"

"Yeah. It's the type of wine to be savored in front of a fireplace."

Her brows furrow. "I'm sorry that I'm messing up your date with the fireplace. Maybe that's why it decided to attack me."

I snort. "At least you succeeded in getting a fire going."

"Yeah." A yawn escapes her lips, and she tries to cover it up with her fist.

"I'll get out of your hair and let you sleep. There should be extra blankets and pillows in the hallway closet. Do you need help with the pullout couch?"

"No, I'm good. Thanks."

I start toward the bedroom but then stop and say, "You never ate dinner. If you're still hungry, feel free to eat the stuff I bought."

"I'm not hungry anymore, but thanks for offering and for lending me your clothes."

"You're welcome." That's my cue to go, but I stay and stare.

"Do you need anything?" she asks.

You.

I shake my head. "No. Good night."

eight

CODY

I try to sleep, but I keep tossing and turning, wondering if Sunshine is sleeping soundly. This has been going on for hours. It's already two in the morning—she must be in dreamland. I toss my legs to the side and get out of bed. I have to use the bathroom, and if I use that chance to check on her, so what?

It's cold as hell outside of the bedroom, and I know why. There's no fire going in the fireplace anymore. How come Sunshine didn't restart it? She must be freezing. I use the bathroom quickly, then see about the fire.

Sunshine is sleeping curled up in a ball, blankets covering her from head to toe. Guilt sneaks inside my chest. She's here turning into an ice sculpture while I'm cozy in the bedroom, thanks to the portable heater. I can be an asshole, but I'm not a heartless monster.

I push the blanket away from her face, and she blinks her eyes open. "Cody? What is it?" she asks groggily.

"You're freezing in here. You can sleep in the bedroom."

"What?"

I touch her face, finding her skin ice cold. "Come on. I don't want you catching a cold."

"Where are you going to sleep?" She sits up.

"I'll stay here."

"Then you'll turn into a popsicle. The fire is bound to go out again."

"Well... we could both sleep in the bedroom. I promise this isn't a ruse to get you to have sex with me."

Unless you want to.

"I didn't think it was." She gets up and wraps the blanket around herself. "Man, I'd kill for some socks. I can barely feel my toes."

"I can give you socks."

"Thank you."

She sighs as soon as she enters the bedroom. "Oh, it feels so nice in here. Which side of the bed do you prefer?"

"I don't have a preference. I usually hog the whole thing."

I expect her to have a snarky response to that, but

she simply picks the left side. She doesn't slide under the duvet though. Instead, she uses the blanket she brought to cover herself and lies on her left side, facing outward.

"You can get under the sheets, you know." I return to the bed, glad that the mattress hasn't gone completely cold.

"I'd rather not. This is fine. What about those socks?"

Shit. Forgot. "Right." I get out of bed and rummage through my duffel in the dark for a pair of woolen socks, going by touch. I usually unpack everything as soon as I arrive, but Sunshine distracted me. I give her the first pair I find, then return to bed.

If I couldn't fall asleep before, with Sunshine next to me, it's impossible. I'm too aware of her presence, of her breathing softly next to me. I shift restlessly, trying to find a good position, but there is none. My arm is out of the sling, but I can't rest on it, which sucks because, to lie on my side, I need to face Sunshine.

She's curled into a ball again, and it looks like she's shivering under her blanket. But it was her decision to not get under the thicker duvet. This room isn't cold, so I shouldn't feel bad about it. Then why the hell do I?

Don't say anything, Cody. She'll think you're trying to score.

I close my eyes and try to fall asleep by focusing on my breathing.

"Cody, are you sleeping?" she asks after a while.

Her voice is soft and sexy but also vulnerable. Hearing it is waking a strange sense of protectiveness in me. I get the physical attraction. She's a knockout. But I'm confused about all the other feelings she's evoking.

"Yes," I lie.

"Is the heater working?"

"It is."

"Are you sure?"

I open my eyes and find her looking at me. I can't make out her face in the darkness, but I can feel her stare. My heart beats faster, and the crazy impulse to pull her closer is almost overwhelming.

"Yes. If you're cold, get under the duvet."

"Oh *fine*."

Shit. I'm really not going to fall asleep now.

"You better be wearing those socks. I don't want any cold feet rubbing against my legs."

She snorts. "You wish I'd rub them against your legs."

Oh, I want you to rub something else, sweetheart.

I start to get aroused and quickly try to think of something else. I cannot get a hard-on while Sunshine is this close to me. The Seattle Saints mascot will do. It's the ugliest version of a St. Bernard dog I've ever seen.

"I can't sleep," she says after a couple minutes.

"Maybe if you stopped talking, you could."

"You don't sound sleepy either."

"It's because some annoying woman won't let me sleep." *And making me question my sanity.*

"Sorry." She sighs loudly, then turns on her side, giving me her back.

She sounds so sad. I feel like a dick for giving her a hard time.

"Why can't you fall asleep?" I ask.

"We don't need to talk about it. You're tired. Go to sleep."

"I can't now. Go on. Maybe your story will bore me, and I'll fall asleep halfway through."

"You say the nicest things."

"It's a gift."

She rolls onto her back and stares at the ceiling. "I can't believe I'm spending what was supposed to be my wedding night with a grumpy stranger."

I get insanely upset about that. I knew she was engaged to someone, but hearing the details bothers me. "Woman, you're wearing my clothes. I'm no longer a stranger."

"You don't deny you're grumpy though." She turns her face toward me.

"No, I wear my grumpy badge with pride. It keeps pesky people away."

"Pesky people like me?"

"You aren't pesky. You're an inconvenience."

Shit. That was harsh.

"Tell me how you really feel, why don't you?" She

doesn't sound hurt. I'd say amused, but I could be wrong. It's hard to tell without being able to see her face clearly. I wish I could though, so I could try to guess what she's feeling.

"Brutal honesty is one of my many qualities." I flash her a toothy smile.

"No wonder you chose to spend Christmas in a secluded cabin in the woods. No one wants you around."

"First of all, you know that ain't true. You heard my sister on the phone. Besides, you also chose to spend Christmas alone in a cabin."

"My circumstances are different." She looks at the ceiling again.

I hesitate for a second, but my curiosity wins. "What happened?"

She sighs heavily. "I walked in on my fiancé screwing one of my bridesmaids an hour before the wedding."

What the actual fuck. I knew something bad had happened but didn't guess that. I'm angry as hell on her behalf, but if I show how livid I am, she might think I'm a little deranged.

"Damn. And here I was thinking you pulled a Julia Roberts move on some poor guy."

She laughs without humor. "I'd never do something terrible like that."

"Did you at least punch his sorry-ass face before you took off?"

"I wish. I was in shock. It turns out he'd been cheating on me with her for a while, and stupid me didn't suspect a thing. I didn't know what to do, so I ran away."

"I'm sorry that happened to you. And for what it's worth, any man who cheats on you is a fucking idiot."

She looks at me. "You don't even know me."

"I wouldn't have cheated on you."

"Right." She sounds disbelieving.

"I've never cheated on anyone. I don't see the point. If my eyes start to wander, then that's a sign the relationship has run its course, so I end it."

"I'm surprised you've had relationships, period."

"Some women dig the grumpy type." I smirk.

She keeps staring at me without saying a thing, then finally mumbles, "I guess."

I want to know what that pause meant. Was she trying to decide if she'd be one of those women? Not that I want to jump into a new relationship anytime soon, especially with someone who clearly wants to get married one day.

I should let the conversation die, but I find myself wanting to know more about her. "What's your plan when you go back home?"

"First order of business is finding a new place to live. We were living together."

Of course they were. This darkness swirling in my chest has nothing to do with jealousy.

"He's probably going to try to win you back." *Shit. Did I sound... bitter?*

"How do you know?"

"I know the type. Whatever you do, don't fall for his bullshit. Even if he promises to never look at another woman, he will cheat again."

"I think that's the most helpful thing you said to me today. But why do you care?"

I roll onto my back, and it's my turn to stare at the ceiling. I don't usually concern myself with other people's love affairs. There's no point because people in love are rarely rational. I'm stumped that I gave Sunshine that piece of advice, but at the same time, I know why.

I don't want her getting back together with her douchey ex, and the possibility of that happening is making me irrationally furious.

nine

. . .

SUNSHINE

I don't know when I fell asleep, but I wake up fast when Cody's arm wraps around my waist and pulls me flush against his body. Is he spooning me? I freeze, not knowing how to react. It's still dark outside, but it could be morning already.

"Cody?" I whisper.

He doesn't answer, so I look over my shoulder and wait until my eyes get used to the gloom. His eyes are closed, and his breathing is even. I don't think he's awake. I face the nightstand again and relax against his body. It feels nice to be this close to him. Even if he doesn't know he's hugging me, a sense of being protected and cherished takes hold of me. Maybe my bruised heart needs the affection.

I close my eyes again and start to fall asleep, but my eyes fly open when Cody's hand disappears underneath my sweatpants. *Oh my God. Oh my God.* Is he having a wet dream? I should push him off me, but when his fingers find my clit over my panties, I let out a whimper instead. This is wrong. He doesn't know he's touching me, but oh, it feels so damn good.

He pushes my panties aside and works my bundle of nerves, flicking his fingers left and right and making me so damn wet that those fingers glide easily. I try to not make a sound while I let him do whatever. I'm behaving badly, but I'm too turned on now to stop him. If he keeps this up, I'll come.

Suddenly, he tenses, and not only does he yank his hand away when I am a second from climaxing, but he also rolls away, creating a gap between our bodies. I feel cold and bereft in an instant. He must have woken up and realized what he was doing. Shit. This is mortifying. I don't want him to know that I consciously let him play with me when he clearly didn't mean to do that. So I pretend to be asleep, hoping he buys my ruse.

"Sunshine?" he whispers.

I don't react, and I force my body to stay relaxed.

A moment later, the mattress dips in one spot and then levels out again. The hinges on the door creak as he opens it and leaves the room.

I don't move for a few seconds, but my heart is beating faster. I'm wide awake now, but I can't get out of bed too soon, or he'll know I was faking sleep. My clit is throbbing, complaining about being denied an orgasm.

Cody closed the door behind him, and I doubt he'll return to bed. Shamelessly, I replace his fingers with mine and finish what he started. It isn't the same—I'm missing the heat of his body behind me. But I'm still super turned on and slick. I imagine it's him running lazy circles around my clit, driving me wild with need. The pressure keeps building until the orgasm hits, making me shake from head to toe. I bite my pillow so I don't scream and keep moving my fingers, trying to make the orgasm last longer. But eventually, the pleasure recedes, and I'm cold and alone again.

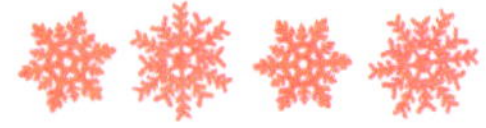

cody

I can't fucking believe I took advantage of Sunshine like that. It doesn't matter that I didn't do it on purpose. I touched her without her consent, and that's not okay. Worst of all, I was dreaming about her. But in the dream, she more than welcomed my caresses. Thank fuck I didn't wake her, but the guilt swirling in my chest is the same.

My cock is as hard as a rock, and normally, I'd take care of it, but I can't bring myself to do it knowing why I have a hard-on. I'm hoping the cold in the living room will do the trick and erase any trace of it.

The microwave clock says it's five past six. It's still dark out, but I'm tempted to go for a walk. I left the bedroom in a hurry, wearing nothing but a pair of sweatpants and a T-shirt. My coat is nice and thick, though, and it's hanging on the peg next to the front door.

The only issue is that I'm barefoot, and my boots are in the bedroom. I can probably walk in to grab them without waking her. I retrace my steps softly, careful not to make a sound. I didn't shut the door completely, and it's open a sliver, allowing me to see Sunshine in bed.

Hell and damn. She's awake and touching herself. The blanket is covering her from the waist down, but it's impossible to mistake the movement of her arm for anything other than what it is. Plus, she's making the most delicious soft sounds.

I freeze. Was she awake when I was touching her and she's now finishing the job? I should turn around and leave, but I'm glued to the floor and, once again, sporting a raging boner. Her arm moves faster, and her breathing becomes shallower. She's close to climaxing.

Unable to stop, I reach inside my pants and curl my fingers around my shaft, then work it at the same pace as Sunshine. It doesn't take long for me to reach the point of no return. I am already worked up, and the visual of Sunshine pleasuring herself is a hell of a turn-on. My balls are tight, ready to explode.

When she rolls on her side and bites her pillow, I lose it. Hot cum covers my fingers as my body convulses, shattering with the release. It's an effort to keep it quiet. I clench my jaw hard until it hurts.

Sunshine sinks into the mattress, her body relaxing. That's my cue to leave lest she see me by the door with my dick in hand. I rush to the bathroom to clean up the mess I made of my sweats. Jesus fucking Christ. I can't believe I jerked off watching her like a damn pervert.

I get rid of the evidence of my despicable act and throw cold water on my face. The scruff on my face is darker; I need a shave, but I can do that later. More than ever, I need to get the hell out of this cabin for a while and sort out my thoughts.

I'm into kinks, voyeurism being one of them, but I've never done anything without my partner being aware of it.

When I walk out of the bathroom, the hallway light is on, and I come face to face with Sunshine, who just walked out of the bedroom. Our gazes lock, and immediately, her cheeks turn bright red. My ears are burning, and I hope she doesn't notice them turning red too.

"Hi," she squeaks.

I can't hold her gaze, afraid she'll see how guilty I

feel, so I carry on toward the living room and say, "If you need to shower, be quick. There's only so much hot water."

"Oh, okay."

Fuck. I'm not only a pervert. I'm a rude pervert.

ten

SUNSHINE

I cry in the shower. I can't attribute my weak moment only to Cody's rudeness, but it is a factor. What the hell did I do now? I can't wait to get out of here and never think about him again. I don't wash my hair because it will take too long, plus I'd have to dry it off before hitting the road. That would mean more delays.

I'd die to brush my teeth, but I make do with rubbing toothpaste over them. It's not the same, but it will take care of morning breath.

I wish I could ignore Cody and just leave, but I need to eat breakfast, and we're sharing the tiniest space. I don't expect to find him in the middle of the kitchen holding a spatula, nor the spread of scrambled eggs, sausage, bacon, and toast on the counter, plus two plates.

"What's this?" I ask.

"My way to say I'm sorry."

My heart does a little somersault, but I don't want him to think I'm a pushover. It's bad enough he knows my fiancé was cheating on me and I had no idea.

"What could you possibly have done to feel sorry about?" I let sarcasm drip over my question.

His eyes are guilty as fuck when he looks into mine. "I was rude."

"No. Really?"

"Do you always mock people when they're trying to apologize?"

I shake my head. "Sorry. I'm just feeling raw."

He cocks an eyebrow, and there's a phantom of a smirk on his lips. I'm not sure why he's reacting that way. It's almost as if he suspects I was playing with myself and got a little chafed from rubbing too hard.

"Why are you looking at me like that?"

"Like what?"

"Like the cat who ate the canary."

The mirth vanishes from his face, and he turns away. "You better eat your food before it gets cold."

"Thanks for cooking. It saves me time. I can't wait to get on the road."

He rubs the back of his neck. "Yeah... about that."

My spine goes taut. "What?"

"You should look outside."

Curious and a little worried, I walk to the nearest window. Everything is covered in snow, and flurries keep falling, creating a thick blanket that makes it impossible to see farther than the cabin's wraparound balcony.

"Please don't tell me we're snowed in." I look at him.

"Fine. I won't."

I step away from the window and press my palm to my forehead. Twelve hours trapped with Cody was enough to make me want to leave, especially after what happened this morning. Now I can't, for God knows how long, and I don't know what to do with myself.

Cody has returned the pullout couch to its original position, and I drop onto it like a sack of potatoes. The fireplace has a healthy fire going too. All and all, this is very cozy, and the breakfast spread looks delicious. But it's clear Cody and I can't coexist without bickering. Never mind my crazy attraction to him. I don't know if I should throttle him or kiss him.

He walks over, carrying a plate full of delicious food and holds it out to me. "Here. Eat. Starving yourself won't change the situation."

I look up. "Maybe it could be a sacrifice to the gods."

He gives me a crooked grin. "Death by starvation would take too long. By then, the snowstorm will have passed."

"Who said anything about *me* dying?" I take the plate from him.

"Oh, I thought that's what you meant by sacrifice. My bad."

I take a bite of eggs and sausage and moan out loud. "This is so good. Who taught you to cook like this?"

"No one. I'm self-taught. I enjoy nice food, and eating out all the time isn't good for the figure." He taps his flat belly. I bet I could shred cheese on those abs.

Stop imagining the guy naked, Sunshine.

"Is that why most hockey players marry before they're thirty? To have someone to take care of them?" The glint of sheer horror in his eyes is almost comical. "What? Is that a wrong assumption?"

"I'm never getting married."

Disappointment rushes through me. I blink fast, more shocked by how I react to his statement than by the statement itself. "Why not?"

He returns to the kitchen. "I don't believe in marriage."

"Okay, but there must be a reason you don't believe in marriage."

He grabs his plate, but instead of sitting next to me on the couch, he brings it to the breakfast nook behind me. "There are many reasons, but I'll give you one. People change, and love fades. Why do you think there are so many divorces?"

"Not all marriages end in divorce. My parents have

been married for thirty years, and they're as in love with each other as they were when they married."

"So you think."

I frown. "I don't think. I've witnessed it with my own eyes."

"I stand by what I said. The number of divorces would be much higher if people weren't so afraid of being alone." He takes a huge bite of his food and chews slowly.

"Well, I want to get married." I return my attention to the food, which is sadly already cold.

"I'm surprised that you, of all people, would want that."

I bristle but don't turn to look at him. "Why? Because my ex-fiancé is a piece of shit?"

"Uh, yeah."

"I picked the wrong guy, that's all." I pierce my food with the fork rather aggressively. Cody is seriously pissing me off.

From the corner of my eye, I watch him walk to the kitchen again. "Why are you trying to murder your food? You know the pig in that sausage is already dead, right?"

I stand up and follow him into the kitchen with my plate half-full. As delicious as the food is, Cody has aggravated me to the point of killing my appetite. "I don't know how we're going to survive the next few days."

His eyes bug out. "What did I do now?"

"If you don't know, I'm not going to explain."

He rolls his eyes. "That's such a 'woman' response."

"What's that supposed to mean?" I glower.

"If you don't know, I'm not going to explain." He throws my retort back at me.

I bite my tongue and count to ten in my head. It's either that or turning to aggression. I'm not a violent person, but Cody is pushing me toward it. "Where's the trash?"

"You're going to throw away my food?" His brows arch.

"I'm no longer hungry."

"Fine. I'll eat it." He grabs my plate, but I hold on to it. "Let it go, Sunshine."

"No. Why do you want to eat my leftovers when there's plenty of food left on the counter?"

"I don't like to waste food." He yanks harder, and the plate slips from my fingers, sending eggs and sausage flying up in the air. "Shit!"

"Look at the mess you made, you jerk!"

"Are you saying this is *my* fault? If you weren't so stubborn, this wouldn't have happened!"

"I'm not stubborn," I grit out, craning my neck to keep glowering at him.

"I'm beginning to see now why your fiancé cheated on you."

My chest hurts as if he punched me. I shuffle back. "I can't believe you said that."

His eyes widen and fill with remorse. "I'm sorry. That was uncalled for."

He's blocking my way, so I shove past him, and he ends up hitting his elbow on the edge of the counter—the elbow attached to the arm in the sling.

"Fuck!" Cody blurts out, hunching over, his face twisting in agony.

"Shit! I'm so sorry. I didn't mean to hurt you."

Cradling his arm, he looks at me, but not with anger flashing in his eyes as I expected. I still see the guilt from before. His brows are furrowed, and his jaw is locked tight. He must be riding the pain, which makes me feel even worse.

"What can I do? Do you have any painkillers or—"

Faster than a cobra, with his good arm, he reaches for the back of my head, pulls me close, and slants his mouth over mine. My lips are already half-open, so his tongue finds mine in an instant and turns me into flames. I curl my fingers around his shirt and let him devour my mouth.

My brain is going haywire. I'm kissing another man less than twenty-four hours after breaking up with my fiancé, and I don't feel an ounce of hesitation. Chad never kissed me with this much passion, not even at the beginning of our relationship. It's clear Cody is a different breed of man. He's wild and possessive, and he's turning me into a puddle without any effort. My heart is beating at breakneck speed, and when he pulls back and looks into my eyes, I want to drown in the depths of his gaze. He keeps my hair wrapped around his hand while he stares as if searching for the answer to an unspoken question.

"Yes," I whisper.

He curls his lips into a sexy grin. "Are you reading my mind now, Sunshine?"

"I don't know. Am I?"

His smile broadens. "Fuck yeah." He releases my hair, then takes my hand and steers me to the bedroom.

I'm giddy, like a teenage girl about to make out with her crush, but I'm hoping for more than kisses. This morning's accident ignited a fire in me, and it won't be extinguished until I get my fill of Cody.

Once there, I jump onto the mattress so I'm taller than him and capture his scruffy face with both hands to kiss him again. He grabs my ass, squeezing it while savoring my mouth with the same urgency as before. I'm light-headed, euphoric beyond measure.

I pull back this time, needing to confess. "This morning... I was awake."

His pupils dilate a little, and his brows arch ever so slightly. "I'm sorry. I didn't know what I was doing."

"I know. But I didn't stop you. I was enjoying what you were doing too much."

"Why didn't you tell me?"

"I was embarrassed."

He touches my face with the tips of his fingers. "You never have to be embarrassed for being horny, gorgeous. Not with me." A dark shadow crosses his eyes and his forehead crinkles.

"What is it?"

"I have to confess something too."

Oh shit. I have the feeling this won't be good. My stomach twists as I wait for him to continue.

"I saw you finishing the job."

My eyes go round and my face heats up like a hot-air balloon. "What?"

"The door wasn't shut all the way, and I saw you. I should have left, but I didn't and I—"

"Did you jerk off while watching me?"

He clenches his jaw hard, and I take that as a sign that he did watch me. I'm not sure how I feel about it.

"Yes. I know it was wr—"

"I don't care that you did it." I take a step back. I should be outraged, but at the same time, what he did was pretty hot. But only because it was him. "If you want, I can do a repeat."

His eyes narrow, turning wolfish. "I'd rather touch you myself, or better yet, taste you instead."

He unhooks the sling and sets it down. Then he pulls off his long-sleeve T-shirt carefully, on account of his arm, revealing the ripped abs I thought he had. They're so much better than my imagination. I keep staring as my desire reaches new heights. I get chills down my spine, and I might climax from appreciating the view.

I want him to look at me the same way I'm looking at him, so I follow suit and get rid of the borrowed sweatshirt that does nothing for my figure. As soon as they're exposed, my nipples turn hard, and goose bumps break out on my skin. Cody freezes, his burning gaze locked on my breasts.

He looks at my face and reaches for my waist, curling his arm around it. "Come here, beautiful."

The bed isn't tall, so my breasts are at the level of his face, and he takes full advantage of that. He captures one nipple, sucking it hard into his hot mouth. I arch my back, threading my fingers through his hair, and moan, "Yes."

He stops sucking and runs lazy circles around it instead, and I don't know which caress I like best. He moves on to my other breast and shows it the same dedication. My panties are already soaked through, and my clit is throbbing in anticipation. I think he'd spend all eternity on my breasts if I didn't yank his hair back and pull him away from them.

"I need your mouth in other places." I kiss him hard, surrendering to the insanity of this moment. I'm about to get railed by a mercurial, sinfully hot hockey player, and I can't help thinking he's the best Christmas gift I could have hoped for. I love the bruising way he kisses me, the fervor of his tongue dancing with mine. I get dizzy, lost in the taste of him.

He bites my lower lip softly while tugging on the elastic band of my sweats. "I want these off."

Two can play at this game. I drop to my knees on the mattress but keep my eyes locked on his as I reach for the front of his pants and rub my hand over his erection. He grabs a fistful of my hair, twisting it tightly around his fist.

"You want a taste, don't you, gorgeous?"

"Yes." I pull his pants down, freeing his cock, and then stare at it, marveling at the sheer size and already imagining how he's going to destroy me with it.

"Go on. Open your gorgeous mouth."

"Patience, big boy." I curl my fingers around the base and lick his length from top to bottom, deliberately slowly.

Narrowing his eyes, Cody tightens his hold on my hair. "Don't tease me, Sunshine."

I raise an eyebrow. "Or what?" I lick his head, tasting the saltiness of precum on my tongue.

"Or I'll take over."

Tendrils of desire roll down my spine and curl at the base. I want him to follow through on his promise, so I keep torturing him, licking his cock as if it's a popsicle while holding his stare.

He yanks my hair a bit harder. "You asked for me. Open your mouth wide."

The pain and his command turn me on even more. I do as he says and swallow his length all the way to the back of my throat. He moves his hips, thrusting hard into my mouth while keeping my head in place. I try to use my tongue to increase his pleasure, but he's relentless, fucking my mouth so fast that it brings tears to my eyes.

"You like that, don't you, sweetheart?" he rasps. "Go on, take it all. Show me you're a good girl."

Since I can't reply, I reach for his tight ass and dig my long nails into his skin, making him hiss.

"Fuck. You take me so well with that filthy mouth of yours, Sunshine."

He grows bigger and harder, and his movements are faster. He's about to come, so I scratch his butt cheeks, hoping the pain will push him over the edge. I want to make him lose control because I'm already spiraling.

He tosses his head back and lets out a guttural sound that's pure male. His cock pulses as his hot seed fills my mouth. I try to swallow it all, but some of it drips down my chin. He looks at me with hooded eyes, his thrusts slowing in pace.

He releases my hair and cups my cheek. "You have no idea how gorgeous you look with your mouth wrapped around my cock, Sunshine."

I pull back, releasing his erection with a wet pop. My jaw hurts a little, but it is worth it just to see him looking at me like that. He wipes the corner of my lips with his thumb, and I can't resist sucking it into my mouth.

He gives me a crooked smile. "You're a naughty girl, aren't you?"

I release his thumb so I can answer him. "I only show my naughty side to bad boys."

He narrows his eyes, leaning down and bringing his face inches from mine. "And how many bad boys have you been with, Sunshine?"

I don't know if this is just play, but he sounds jealous, and the notion sends a thrill of excitement down my back. I hesitate, considering lying to push his buttons, but in the end, I opt for the truth.

"Just one. You."

eleven

. . .

CODY

Jealousy spreads through my chest when Sunshine tells me she only shows her naughty side to bad boys. I don't want to picture her with anyone but me, even though it's stupid to suffer from retroactive jealousy over a woman I just met. But when she confesses I'm the only bad boy she's been with, I can't help feeling smug.

"Good. Now I want to see your pretty little cunt." I nudge her back, and she falls on the mattress. "Take your pants off."

Her cheeks turn bright pink, but her blue eyes are pure fire. Holding my gaze, she rolls the thick material down her long legs, revealing a pair of white lacy panties. I see red again, knowing they were meant for another man. Before she can take those off too, I grab one of the sides and yank, tearing the fabric.

Her eyes go wider. "Why did you do that? These were my only pair."

"You won't need them, gorgeous. I plan to keep you naked for the entire duration of our stay."

She glares, furrowing her brows together. "And when I go home?"

I join her on the mattress, opening her legs wide and kneeling between them. "You can go commando. I like the idea of your bare pussy rubbing against my sweatpants." I lower my body, leaning on my right forearm and bringing my mouth to her flat stomach. Her body tenses a little, so I look up. "Are you nervous, Sunshine?"

"No."

I run my tongue across her belly, right under her navel, while watching her reaction. Her lovely breasts rise and fall faster, and her luscious lips part. I maintain eye contact as I move lower, planting wet kisses on the way. I'm hard again, ready to fuck her into oblivion, but not before I obliterate her with my tongue first.

I break the connection to look at her bare pussy. "Such a beauty." I flatten my palm against it first, massaging the entire area. Sunshine's breathing becomes shallower and her legs tense.

"It's okay, gorgeous. I'll make you feel good." I part

her folds with my finger, revealing her pink nub, and flick my tongue across it, making Sunshine's hips buckle. "Shhh, it's okay, darling, I'm just getting started."

I lick with gusto, loving how velvety she is against my tongue and sweet at the back of my throat. Her taste is addictive, and I can't stop eating her out. The sounds she's making put my libido in overdrive. I pull back to glance at her face. Her eyes are closed and she's clutching the sheets in a vise hold.

"Eyes on me, Sunshine."

She looks at me, her blue eyes shining with need. Women have looked at me with desire plenty of times, but none of them stared with undiluted passion and curiosity. I suspect no other man has made her feel this good. It makes me want to fulfill all her fantasies, make her come so hard she'll never want anyone else.

Holding her gaze, I insert two fingers in her drenched pussy, curling them a little to search out her sweet spot. She gasps loudly, and I know I've hit the mark.

"Make that sound again."

"What sound?" she whispers.

"Moan for me, gorgeous. Beg for more." I keep pumping my fingers in and out while pressing my thumb over her clit.

"Please, Cody, give me more."

I push four fingers inside and then bring my mouth

back to her clit for a double assault. She's moving her hips now, trying to fuck my fingers instead of the other way around. When her walls tighten around them, I suck her clit into my mouth hard, and she breaks apart.

"Fuck me!" she yells. "Oh my God. Don't stop."

I keep working her with my tongue and fingers, loving the flavor of her orgasm. I've eaten a lot of pussies, but none of them compared to hers. I already know I'm coming back for seconds and thirds... as many times as she allows me.

My cock is as hard as it can be, and I could come again by simply watching her unravel in front of me. I clench my butt cheeks, trying to avoid that.

When I sense her body relaxing, I ease off her pussy and kiss her inner thighs but keep my fingers moving slowly.

"I can't..." She closes her legs, then tries to roll onto her side, forcing me to pull my hand away too.

"Don't tell me you're done, beautiful."

She turns to me, showing me her flushed cheeks and swollen lips. "Fuck no, I'm not done."

I smile from ear to ear. "Good. 'Cause I have plans for you."

Arching an eyebrow, she asks, "Oh yeah? What?"

Still smiling, I wink at her. "You'll have to wait and see."

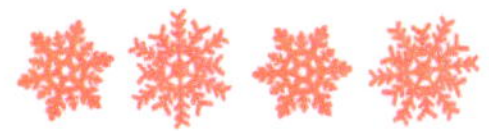

sunshine

I'm boneless, and yet I want more. Cody has turned me into an insatiable woman. I never knew I could have such an earth-shattering orgasm. His tongue and fingers drove me insane, and I can't wait to see what he'll do next.

I watch him jump off the bed and grab a box of condoms from his duffel bag. My eyebrows rise. "Were you expecting company here?"

He smirks. "I always have condoms on me. You never know when they'll be needed."

A sad feeling pierces my chest. I should have known a guy who looks like Cody would have plenty of women interested in him. And no one gets to be a god in bed without a lot of practice.

"What's wrong, gorgeous?" he asks.

"Nothing."

"Are you upset that I had condoms in my bag?"

"No, of course not."

He takes a condom from the box and rips open the wrapper with his teeth. He keeps looking at me as he rolls the condom down his cock, and I'm torn between holding his stare and letting my gaze travel south. I opt for maintaining eye contact. Once protection is in place, he joins me in bed, getting comfortable between my legs and leaning on his right forearm. His erection presses against my pussy, reminding me that I still want to get railed by him. Besides, it doesn't matter if he's a Casanova. I'll never see him again after we leave the cabin.

He traces my face with his fingers, keeping his eyes locked on mine. "I like to fuck, and I'm very good at it, but I'm not a player, and I've never cheated on anyone."

Warmth spreads through my chest, which is ridiculous. His confession shouldn't affect me so much. "You don't need to explain your life choices to me."

"True. But when I fuck you, I need you to surrender to the moment completely, without any doubts in your mind."

I bring my knees up and cross my legs at the ankles behind his ass. "I want you, Cody, like I've never wanted anyone else in my life. I want—no, I *need* you to fuck me until I can't feel my body anymore. I want to forget the world exists while we're here."

His sinful mouth breaks into a grin. "I plan to do just that, beautiful."

With a rotation of his hips, his cock slides into me, gliding easily. I let out a little gasp, not used to his size. He's stretching me in the most delicious way, and I press my heels against his ass, urging him to fill me to the hilt.

"Fuck, Sunshine. You're so tight," he whispers

against my lips before claiming them in a long and sensual kiss.

He starts slowly, pulling his cock almost all the way out, only to slam back in. With every thrust, tingles of pleasure run down my spine, and the pressure between my legs spreads. Our mouths stay fused together even when his pace increases. The bed shakes, and the wrought iron headboard bangs against the wall.

Cody leans back suddenly and tosses my leg over his right shoulder. My hips lift off the mattress, and this new angle proves to be even better than before. As much as I crave his kisses, I love my current view. The veins on his neck bulge, and his chest and abs flex as he fucks me faster and faster. Never mind his gorgeous face, twisted in pleasure. I'll never forget how sexy he looks now.

I'm not far from climaxing, but when he reaches for my neck and squeezes a little while he pounds into me, it sends me over the edge, and I shatter into a million pieces. I'd have shouted a million yeses if he wasn't constricting my airway. I've heard of breath play but never dared to ask Chad to try. Holy *shit*. I had no idea how good it would feel.

Cody releases my neck and leans forward again, keeping my leg over his shoulder, and slants his mouth over mine. Thank fuck for all the years I took ballet, or this stretch wouldn't have been possible. His tongue takes possession of mine with a new fervor, and the way he keeps moving faster and faster turns me feral. I scratch his back while I'm assaulted by another wave of pleasure.

Cody seems to grow larger inside me, and when his entire frame shakes, I flex my internal walls in response.

"Fuck, Sunshine. You feel so good, so damn good." He kisses my neck, sucking and biting it, while he comes, hard.

He keeps fucking me even after the tremors in his body subside, and it's another minute or so before he stops completely.

We're both breathing hard, and our bodies are covered in sweat. I close my eyes, loving the weight of his body on mine. This has been the most intense sexual experience of my life, and it makes me realize… I've been missing out.

twelve

. . .

CODY

I can't move, so I just lie there, still sheathed inside Sunshine, as I catch my breath, careful to keep most of my weight off her. She runs her nails down my back softly, a caress that tickles, making me chuckle.

"Are you ticklish, Cody?"

I lean back and lie, "No."

Her eyes shine with amusement. "We'll see about that."

She goes for the kill and tickles me with intent now, making me laugh uncontrollably. I have to roll off her to escape her devilish touch. "Stop it, woman."

"No way." She straddles me, giving me a great view

of her luscious breasts. "Let's see what other weak spots you have."

My neck is her first target, and hell, it's impossible to hide my reaction from her. I lift my good shoulder, trying to protect the area. Between laughter, I beg her to stop, but at the same time, I don't because she's laughing with me, and the sound is infectious. She has a lovely laugh, and for the first time since meeting her, I don't see a shadow of sadness in her eyes.

I could easily push her off me, but I beg instead, "Please, have mercy."

She goes still, but the amusement on her face remains. "Who knew the mighty Cody Fairchild had a weak spot?"

I sit up, bringing my face inches from hers. "And that's the only weak spot you'll find. What about you, gorgeous? Any weaknesses?" I kiss her neck right below her ear, and she immediately melts into me.

"No," she replies with a throaty sigh.

Shit. I lied. I have another weakness, one I didn't know I possessed. Making Sunshine unravel is quickly becoming my kryptonite. My hard-on is back, which is an issue because I'm still wearing a loaded condom.

I lean back and look into her eyes. "I think you're lying, Sunshine. But don't worry, I'll find it."

She smirks. "Good luck. How's your arm, by the way?"

I snort. "*Now* you remember I'm injured?"

Guilt shines in her eyes. "I'm sorry. I... it was easy to forget when you were..."

"A beast in bed?" I arch a brow, trying to keep my grin from becoming a broad smile. "My arm is fine, Sunshine. It's my shoulder that's messed up." Her cheeks turn bright red, and she can't hold my stare. Her eyes drop to my neck, but I need to look into her eyes, so I pinch her chin between my forefinger and thumb, bringing her face up again. "You aren't feeling regretful, are you?"

Her eyebrows meet her hairline. "What? No. Why would you think that?"

"Considering why you wound up here, it isn't a far-fetched assumption, is it?"

She pushes my hand away, lifting her chin proudly. Her eyes burn with the same fire that made me lose control and kiss her in the kitchen. "I have no regrets."

I stare for a few more seconds but see nothing but unwavering determination in her gaze. "Good. Do you want to shower first? I can wait."

"It's okay. You go ahead." She looks down. "You're leaking."

I follow her line of sight and see what she means. Cum is escaping the condom. "Right. I won't take long."

"Don't worry about me. I'm not going anywhere." She lies on her back, and her long red hair fans around her head like a halo. She looks like a fucking goddess from a Renaissance painting.

I have to force myself to walk out of the bedroom. I never thought I'd wish for a snowstorm to last longer, but I do now.

sunshine

The moment I'm alone in the room, the reality of what I just did hits me. I slept with another man—no, I fucked another man's brains out. I loved every minute of it, but sadness takes hold of me. Chad was supposed to be my forever, but instead, he was railing my friend on the side.

The urge to cry returns, but before I start bawling my eyes out, I jump out of bed and get dressed. I won't let that dirtbag ruin my weekend. I find my phone so I can call my parents like I promised. Wishful thinking. There's no reception in the cabin. The snowstorm must have fucked with the cell phone towers. Great.

Maybe I'll get reception outside. I walk out of the room, determined to brave the cold weather in my sweats. Maybe Cody won't mind if I borrow his jacket.

I hear music coming from the bathroom and stop in my tracks. I'm shocked when I recognize "Anti-Hero" and Cody singing along to it. *Oh my God.* The sex-god hockey player is a Swiftie. If what's happening here wasn't strictly a rebound situation, and I wasn't nursing a broken heart, I might fall for the guy.

I glance at the kitchen and see the mess of sausage and scrambled eggs we left behind on the floor. Crap. I better clean that up. Even though it wasn't completely my fault, I hate messes, and I'm not doing anything right now.

It doesn't take long to clean the floor, and I go ahead and put the leftover food away, but not before I eat more of it. Cody is still in the bathroom, but the water in the shower is no longer running. I don't want to think too much about what he's doing in there.

With time to kill, I inspect the contents of the closet in the hallway. My jaw drops. I can't believe the treasure I find inside: Christmas decorations! I have been prepared to pretend this isn't Christmas weekend, but I can't ignore it now. Sure, it sucks I'm not spending the holiday with my family, but I can bring some Christmas spirit to this cabin.

The box doesn't contain much, just a few strands of green and silver tinsel, tree ornaments, and colorful lights. Since we don't have a tree to decorate, I leave the ornaments in the box. The tinsel I drape over the fireplace mantel, and the lights I hang by the windows, using the curtain pegs.

I've just finished my work when Cody joins me in the living room. "What fresh hell is this?"

"Uh, what?" I turn to him and notice he's clean-shaven. God, he's even yummier now, and kissing him won't rub me raw.

While I'm admiring him, he's glowering at the lights. "Where did you find Christmas decorations?"

"In the hallway closet. Why?"

"I hate Christmas." He veers for the kitchen and freezes. "You cleaned up?"

I'm annoyed by his comment, so I can't help my sarcastic answer. "No, Santa's elves did."

He glances at me with narrowed eyes. "It seems I haven't fucked the sass out of you yet."

I cross my arms. "You never will, no matter how many orgasms you give me."

He smirks, his previous irritation gone from his eyes. "We'll see about that."

And just like that, my annoyance goes away too. How can I be mad at him when he looks at me like that? Besides, I don't care that he hates Christmas. It's his loss, not mine.

I clear my throat. "I wanted to call my folks to let them know I'm okay, but we don't have any service in the cabin."

"We can try outside, but we might need to get to higher ground." He looks at my clothes. "You need warmer clothes."

"No shit, Sherlock."

"Sassy girl, don't provoke me. I'll bend you over that counter and fuck all your holes if you keep going."

My eyes widen, and adrenaline spikes in my veins. I've never been fucked in the ass before, but mainly because none of my previous boyfriends were interested. Losing my *other* virginity to Cody is something I can't resist.

"Is that a promise?" I arch an eyebrow.

He takes a step forward, and my stomach flutters. Is he going to follow through? But instead of shortening the distance between us, he points in the bathroom's direction. "Get in the shower, Sunshine. We can try to call your parents after."

I usually hate being bossed around, but I don't have a problem when Cody does it. Why is that? Is it because he's being considerate and thinking about helping me? Or maybe I do enjoy being dominated by a man when it feels like it's foreplay that will lead to mind-blowing sex.

"Fine. You better not have used all the hot water."

"We shall see. I know I'll pay for it if I did."

"Oh, you will."

My reply amuses him. His eyes are dancing with mirth. "I'm curious about your punishment methods though."

"Fuck around and find out."

I stride toward the bathroom so he doesn't have the chance to reply. I'm feeling pretty smug about having the final word. I have a feeling Cody doesn't allow that to happen often.

In the shower, I think about his threat and then begin to fantasize about it. I'm aroused again and tempted to take care of my situation myself. But in the end, I focus on washing my hair before the water turns cold. I'll let Cody take care of my other needs.

thirteen

· · ·

SUNSHINE

I quickly find out it was a mistake to wash my hair. There isn't a blow dryer in sight. Shit. Because the cabin is super nice and luxurious inside, I was tricked into believing I was in a hotel room. I'm an idiot. My long hair will take forever to dry, and there's no chance I'll venture outside with a wet head.

I put on Cody's sweats again—sans underwear this time since he destroyed my only pair—and untangle my hair using Cody's brush. I make sure to leave no strands in it. I've had my share of ex-boyfriends bitching about finding my hair everywhere, even though I'm always careful to keep everything clean.

I wrap a towel around my head and glance at my

reflection in the bathroom mirror. I sigh. His clothes are far too big for me. I want to look cute and sexy, especially now that I crossed the line with Cody. I'd give anything to have my own clothes. Also, going commando while I'm wearing his pants feels oddly intimate. Which is stupid. He's been inside me for crying out loud.

I wonder what he's doing. I can't hear anything outside the bathroom. He'd better not have taken my Christmas decorations down. When I return to the living room, I find it empty. Is he in the bedroom? I get oddly excited that he might be waiting for me naked in bed, but he's not there either.

My chest tightens. What if he left? I hurry to the front window. It's still snowing, but not with the same intensity as before. His truck is out there, parked next to my car. The vise hold worry had around my heart slackens. But if he didn't go home, where the hell is he? Maybe he went on a hike to see if he could get a signal? Annoyance replaces worry. I didn't take *that* long in the shower. Why didn't he wait for me?

Fine. I can go on my own. I just need to get my hair dry first. I throw a couple more pieces of wood in the fireplace and sit in front of it, getting toasty warm in an instant.

My mind wanders as I watch the flames dance. Alone in the cabin without Cody distracting me, it's impossible not to think about Chad and Monica. When the memory of them screwing comes to the forefront of my mind, I wait for the nausea to hit, but all I get is a deep feeling of disappointment… in myself. How could I not see Chad's duplicity? I never suspected a thing. He was an attentive fiancé, always making sure I was happy. We never fought about anything and naively, I thought that was a sign that I'd found the perfect guy. But maybe he went out of his way to make me happy because he felt guilty, not because he loved me. Or maybe he did love me but couldn't commit to a single person. Regardless, I was wrong about him and our relationship, and now I'm questioning every decision I've ever made.

Ugh, stop doing that, Sunshine. You'll drive yourself crazy.

I need to get out of this cabin. I touch my hair, finding it still damp. Hell. It'll have to be good enough. I jump to my feet and head to the bedroom. Since Cody left me alone without saying a word, I don't feel bad about raiding his duffel bag. I do hope I don't find anything inside that will turn me off.

The sweatshirt is only good enough to stay indoors. I need more layers. I grab the thickest wool sweater he has and put it on, then I find a matching hat to go with it and a scarf. Sadly, he didn't bring an extra coat, so the blanket will have to do as the extra protection. I don't see another pair of boots, either, but even if he had brought a spare pair, my feet would probably swim in them.

It's time to improvise.

I keep the socks on and put on my ruined wedding shoes. It's a tight fit, but the satin shoes are softer after getting wet. I cover them with garbage bags, tying them tight around my ankles. When I look at my reflection in the full-length mirror in the bedroom, I burst out laughing. Oh my God. I look ridiculous.

I grab my phone and take selfies. I don't know if I'll ever show them to anyone, but I need to capture this moment of insanity.

Not wanting to ruin my phone by getting it wet, I put it in a ziplock bag. I gotta say, Cody's sister keeps this cabin well stocked with basic supplies. Even with the mix-up, I'll give her a five-star review that has nothing to do with how good her brother is in bed.

With the blanket tied around my shoulders, I open the front door and step outside. "Holy shit. It's cold."

My teeth start to chatter immediately. I debate going back inside. But it has stopped snowing. This is my best chance to find higher ground. "You can do this, Sunshine."

I'm careful not to slip and fall down the steps. Perhaps the garbage bags over my shoes wasn't the best idea. But once I reach the fluffy snow, they aren't as slippery. However, I soon realize wearing the wedding shoes is a mistake. They aren't helping to keep my feet warm, and they're delaying my progress. They have to go.

I can't sit down, or I'll get my clothes wet. It's time to test my balance. Standing on one leg, I untie the first bag and take my shoe off, then toss it aside. I put the bag back on and repeat the same process with my left foot, now I can walk without fear of falling and breaking my neck.

The cabin is surrounded by evergreen trees, but it's not a dense forest, nor is the hill very steep. I take my phone out and check if I get anything. No signal, but I'm hopeful. I start my trek, hoping the weather will stay snow-free for as long as I'm outside.

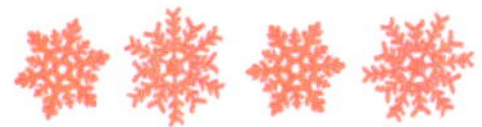

My legs are burning by the time I reach the highest point of my hike. Checking the time on my phone, I see that it took me half an hour, but it feels like I've been walking forever. My breathing is labored, and I'm so cold I can barely feel my extremities. But the effort is worth it because I have a signal.

I call my mother right away, praying she'll pick up the phone. It'll suck if they miss my call.

"Sunshine? Oh my God, dear, we were so worried."

Guilt pierces my chest, making me teary-eyed. "Hi Mom."

"Where have you been? We've been calling for hours and getting nothing but your voice mail."

"I'm sorry. I lost signal in the cabin."

"Hold on. Let me put you on speaker so your father can hear you."

"Hey, honey. How are you?" he asks.

"I'm fine, Dad. You guys don't need to worry about me." I try to keep my voice steady so they don't notice I'm sad.

"We'll always worry, Sunshine," Mom replies. "The weather has taken a turn for the worse. Are you okay?"

"Yeah. I won't be able to drive back down until the storm passes, but I'm fine otherwise."

"Honey, give me the address and I'll come get you with my truck," Dad says.

Shit. I can imagine my father arriving at the cabin and finding Cody there. He'd have a cow for more reasons than one. First, he wouldn't appreciate that I'm trapped in a one-bedroom cabin with a strange man. And second, he'd probably be starstruck. He's a huge Seattle Saints fan.

I wish I'd paid more attention to the games on TV. Now I'm curious about what kind of player Cody is. I don't even know what position he plays. I bet he gets into a lot of fights.

"Sunshine? Are you still there?" Mom asks.

Shit. I totally spaced out, thinking about Cody. "Yeah. I'm here. Dad, you don't need to come get me. I'll be fine. Truly. Being cut off from the world is exactly what I need right now."

"I don't like it, but I understand," he replies.

"That worthless piece-of-shit Chad came by the house looking for you," Mom chimes in.

I become anxious in an instant, but I guess it's better than being hopeful. It means there's no chance I'll be one of those women who forgives their cheating partners.

"He did? What did he say?"

"We don't know. Your father sic'd the dogs on him."

A bubble of laughter goes up my throat. Chad has always been terrified of our family dogs, Chip and Dale. They're a pair of Chihuahuas, the smallest little buggers but psychotic.

"I can't believe I missed that."

"Oh, I got it on camera. I'll send it to you."

Immediately, I reject the idea. "It's okay, Mom. I'm not ready to see any videos of Chad, no matter how funny they are."

"Of course, honey. We'll watch it when you're ready," Dad replies, then laughs. "It was funny as shit."

It starts to snow again, which means my time is up. I have to get back to the cabin before I turn into a human popsicle.

"I have to go. I'll talk to you later, okay?"

"Okay. Bye, sweetheart. We love you," Mom replies.

"I love you too."

I feel so much better now that I talked to them, but at the same time, guilt is swirling in my chest. I hate that I'm worrying my parents, and on top of that, I'm ruining Christmas for them. Now that I'm over the shock of catching Chad with Monica, I can see how selfish I was to hide in the cabin. If it weren't for the snow keeping me trapped, I'd go home today.

But then… no more Cody.

I branch snapping nearby spooks me and sends my heart up my throat. I turn around too fast and lose my footing. A yelp leaves my mouth as I fall face-first in the snow. It's so cold. *Son of a bitch.*

Now I can hear the distinct sound of boots crunching in the snow. I scramble to get back on my feet, wiping my face at the same time because I can't see anything.

"There you are." Cody's baritone voice reaches me.

"Jesus, you scared me."

"What are you doing up here?"

"What do you think? Trying to find a signal. Where have you been?"

His eyes widen, and they're the only thing I can see on his face. His hat is covering his brows, and he has a thick scarf covering his jaw and nose.

"What do you mean? I went into town. I left you a note on the kitchen counter."

"I didn't see a note." I wipe my pants, but it's no use. I'm already wet.

"What the hell are you wearing?" He sounds angry now.

"Whatever I could find."

"Are you *trying* to die of hypothermia?"

"Stop chiding me. You're not my dad." I start walking, hoping movement will help with the cold. But my muscles are locking up. Shit, maybe I'm already freezing for real.

"If I were, I'd give you a good spanking." He follows me, quickly reaching my side. "For fuck's sake. Are you wearing *garbage bags* as makeshift boots?"

"If you didn't pack so sparingly, I'd be wearing a pair of yours." My retort would be more effective if I didn't slip and almost fall again. Cody reaches for my arm and prevents that from happening.

"You're a menace to yourself."

"I don't need your assistance." I try to yank my arm free, but he holds me tighter.

"Oh, honey. You do." Before I have time to react, Cody flexes his knees, lifts me off the ground using only one arm, and tosses me over his shoulder as if I weigh nothing.

"What the hell! Put me down."

"Sorry, Sunshine. You're too slow, and in case you failed to notice, it's snowing heavily again. We need to get back to the cabin as quickly as possible."

"You're going to get us both hurt! What if you slip? You can't use your left arm to hold on to anything."

"I'm not going to slip, and even if I do, I won't fall."

I would continue to argue, but I don't want to distract him. He won't put me down until we reach the cabin, no matter how much I irritate him. It's best if he remains focused on the trail. But when we're back in the cabin… that's another story.

fourteen

. . .

SUNSHINE

We make it back to the cabin in record time, but enduring Cody's fast pace while my stomach is pressed against his hard shoulder is hell. I'm probably bruised.

He dumps me on the couch and orders, "Take your clothes off."

"You seriously think I want to fuck you now?"

He removes his coat and hat, then turns to me. "I'm not in the habit of screwing corpses, and that's what you'll be if you don't get out of your wet clothes and get your body temperature up."

Jesus, I'm so riled up that I blocked the fact that I'm freezing. But I don't want to undress in front of him when I'm still mad. Besides, the fire in the fireplace isn't burning as high. What I need is a hot shower, so I run to the bathroom and turn on the water to let it warm up. Taking an ice-cold shower would defeat the purpose.

The water is getting hot, so I quickly strip off the clothes, which have frozen solid. Even my hair is frozen, so I have to get it wet again. I expect to find relief, but when the hot jets hit my cold skin, it's painful. I grimace when I notice how blue my toes are. Shit. I hope I didn't get frostbite.

I stay under the water without moving until I'm completely thawed and the water begins to turn cold. The bathroom is foggy, like a sauna. I don't have anything to wear, so the towel will have to do, but I need to borrow new clothes from Cody, and that sucks. I don't want to ask him for another favor while I'm still annoyed.

In hindsight, he saved me from a potentially harmful situation. I don't know how long it would have taken me to return to the cabin on my own. *Ugh.* Even though he acted like a caveman, I have to thank him.

Maybe that'd be an excellent way to disarm him. He's expecting me to give him a hard time. A smile blossoms on my lips. I can be humble and grateful... and end up on top.

Cody must have fed the fire because it's much warmer in the living room. He's sitting in front of the fireplace, holding a glass in his hand. I'm not sure what he's drinking.

He turns and gives me an elevator glance. "I see you didn't lose any toes."

"Nope. Thank you for getting me back to the cabin so quickly."

He cocks an eyebrow. "Are you all right? Did you hit your head in the shower?"

"Do you find it so hard to believe that I might be thankful for what you did?"

"Our past has made me leery." He smirks, then hides his amusement behind his glass. I see the color of his drink—it's either whiskey or cognac. Cognac would probably be a good idea.

As if reading my mind, he says, "There's a glass of cognac with your name on it on the counter."

I pivot and find the glass next to a piece of paper. Upon closer inspection, I see it's the note Cody left for me.

Going to town to check if any stores are open. I should be back in an hour.

"What did you need in town?" I ask, lifting my gaze from the note.

"You'll see in the bedroom." He faces the fireplace again and brings the glass to his lips.

Curious, I head to the bedroom and find several shopping bags on the bed. I look inside the closest one and pull out a thick, dark-red sweater dress.

"What…" I can't believe what I'm seeing.

Cody went to town to buy *me* clothes. Besides the dress, he got me some thick leggings, a pair of winter boots, socks, flannel pj's, and underwear. My face is in flames, and my heart is so full of gratitude that I might actually cry. I want to kiss him until I'm sick of it.

I put on the red dress and leggings, then cover my feet with the long, thick socks he got me. I try on the boots, and I'm shocked that they fit. The dress hugs my curves, and I finally feel like myself.

I'm once again on the verge of tears. It's the whole kindness-from-strangers thing getting to me. That must be it. Although, technically, Cody isn't really a stranger anymore, and maybe because of that, his gesture is even more meaningful.

I suck in a sharp breath and tell my reflection in the mirror, "Pull yourself together, woman."

The pep talk works to keep me from crying, but my pulse still beats at an accelerated pace, and the fluttering in my belly can't be ignored. I'm a little nervous about being in Cody's presence now, which is insane. We're strangers who were forced into close proximity and succumbed to our undeniable physical attraction to one another. This sense of jumpy giddiness is ridiculous.

Maybe I need more orgasms.

Before I return to the living room, I take a couple of condoms from the box in the nightstand and stick them inside my socks because I don't have any pockets.

Cody hasn't moved from his spot on the couch. I grab my glass from the kitchen counter before joining him. He glances at me, and even though his face remains serious, I see appreciation shining in his eyes.

"Thank you for the clothes. You didn't need to buy them for me."

"I didn't bring enough of my own to share. They fit."

And that's probably the closest thing to a compliment I'll get from him.

"Yeah." I glance at the boots. "How did you know my shoe size?"

"Your wedding shoes. I checked before I left. Why did you toss them in the snow, by the way?"

"They were a nuisance, so I got rid of them."

I sit on the couch but keep space between us and remove the boots before bringing my knees up.

"Are you still cold?" he asks.

"No. I'm fine. I just like to sit like this." I take a sip of the cognac, and the warmth from the spirits spreads through my body. Closing my eyes, I relax against the back of the couch.

"Was your trek through the snow worth it, at least?"

I open my eyes again and peek at him. His brows are tense, and his jaw is locked tight. I don't know why he's so angry. "Yeah. I managed to talk to my folks. They were worried, so I'm glad I took the risk."

"You're close to them."

It's not a question, but I still say, "Yeah. How about you?"

"What about me?" He takes a sip of his drink.

"Are you close to your parents?"

"No."

His answer is curt but loaded with meaning. "You're close to your sister though. That's something."

"When you have shitty parents, you either bond with your sibling or perish alone."

My stomach clenches painfully. "I'm sorry."

He looks me in the eye. "Why? I turned out fine."

I laugh, thinking he's joking, but he remains serious. "Oh, you mean that."

His brows furrow together. "How could you possibly know what kind of person I am?"

"You're right. I don't. But I can guess a few things. You hide behind this tough guy facade, but you're a softy at heart."

"I'm not a softy," he grumbles, but it lacks conviction.

"You drove all the way into town during a snowstorm to buy me clothes, and you don't even like me that much."

"Where did you get the notion that I don't like you?"

My eyes widen. "Uh... are you saying you do?"

"When I got back and you were gone, I was worried. You didn't even leave a note, damn it."

"I thought you left to find a signal without me!"

"I wouldn't just take off without telling you where I was going. I'm not an asshole."

I narrow my eyes.

"Okay, I'm not *that* much of an asshole," he amends.

"I'm sorry I didn't leave a note," I say. "I honestly didn't think you'd care where I went."

Cody surprises me by cupping my cheek. "If we're being honest, I didn't expect to care so much."

His green eyes are so earnest and open that they reel me in. The giddiness from before returns with a vengeance, and my heart is beating fast and loud. Unable to resist his pull, I lean closer and place a soft kiss on his lips. I begin to ease away, but he slides his hands to the back of my head and grabs a fistful of my hair before slanting his lips over mine. His tongue coaxes my lips open possessively and hungrily, and my entire body burns from the inside out. Who needs fire when this man's mouth can stir an inferno inside of me?

I break the kiss because I'm still holding the cognac glass. "Hold on."

Cody already put his own glass aside. I set mine on the floor and barely have time to sit straight before he attacks my mouth again.

He keeps his hand on my cheek while he kisses me so passionately I'm melting like ice cream on a summer day. I want to feel his skin against mine again, surrender to his electrifying caresses. My hands slip under his sweater and T-shirt, and Cody moans against my mouth.

"You're not ticklish here too, are you?" I whisper.

"No," he groans. "Your fingers are cold."

I glide them across his taut abs, feeling goose bumps form on his skin. "They'll warm up soon."

"Help me with the sling."

"Okay." I forgot about that little detail. "How's your shoulder?"

"I don't want to talk about my shoulder right this second." He kisses my chin, then continues peppering kisses down my neck, making my skin crackle with desire.

I throw my head back, closing my eyes. "Cody... I thought you needed help with your sling."

"I can't resist you, gorgeous. You taste so damn good."

"I want to taste you too."

He leans back, his lips already curled into a crooked smile. "Oh yeah? Where?"

I reach behind his neck to release the sling's clasp, and as I return to my side of the couch, I make sure our eyes are locked when I say, "Everywhere."

His eyes widen, but before he pounces again, I pull his sweater and T-shirt up, helping him undress. The action messes up his hair a little, making him look even sexier. I run my thumb over his lips. "You're so handsome. Isn't it illegal for hockey players to be this attractive?"

He chuckles. "I've never heard that rule before." He grabs my wrist and sucks my thumb into his mouth, making me hiss. I didn't expect to feel this much pleasure from a simple gesture.

I pull my hand back and straddle him, needing to rub my aching clit against his shaft. Who knew him sucking my thumb would turn me wild?

Our mouths crash together again in a tangle of tongues. I work my hips, grinding my pussy against his erection. God, I haven't done this since high school—I forgot how amazing it feels.

"If you're going to torture me like that, Sunshine, take off your clothes. I want to feel your naked cunt against my cock. I want your juices all over me."

The snug dress has already bunched up around my waist, so I just grab the hem and whip it off. My nipples become hard in an instant, and Cody's gaze drops to them. He leans forward, and I know exactly what's on his mind. But I slide off his lap and stand out of his reach.

"Where are you going?" He looks at me like a little boy who was denied candy.

"You told me to get naked." I take off my socks, then the leggings and underwear follow.

Cody unbuttons his jeans, and I drop to my knees

and help him out of them. His cock springs free, making my mouth water. I want to suck him again, but he gets up from the couch and stands behind me. "Brace your arms against the couch, beautiful, and lift that pretty ass for me."

I look over my shoulder. "What are you up to?"

He drops to his knees, his dick as hard as a rock. I remember the condoms in my sock, and I'm about to tell him, but he leans forward and inserts two fingers inside my pussy, making me lose my train of thought.

"Feel how drenched you already are for me, gorgeous, and I haven't even started yet."

"Cody..."

"Tell me how much you want my cock inside your pussy, Sunshine." He inserts another finger and continues to thrust them in and out, driving me insane with need.

"More than I want anything else in the world."

He keeps fingering me, and it feels fucking amazing. I close my eyes for a moment, trying my hardest to not collapse on the floor. My legs are already shaking, turning into jelly. I'm not prepared when Cody's tongue finds my other hole, sending an entirely new sensation rippling through me. Holy shit.

He rims the sensitive skin around my hole, drawing a ragged moan from me. "Cody... *please...*"

"Please what? If you want me to bury my cock deep in your tight peach hole, you need to say it out loud."

"Yes, I want you to fill all my holes."

He runs his warm tongue up my spine, then whispers in my ear, "That's the right answer, beautiful."

"I... I've never done it before."

Cody seems to tense behind me, and he doesn't breathe a word. I fear I may have ruined things. Why did I have to confess it was my first time getting fucked in the ass?

"Thanks for letting me know, Sunshine." He kisses me below my ear. "I'll be gentle."

fifteen

. . .

CODY

Sunshine has been a surprise in more ways than one. She's brave and feisty, though I can see she's holding back a world of hurt. The biggest surprise is how, without effort, she makes me want to do nice things for her. Braving all that fucking snow in the hopes any of the shops in town were open so I could buy her some clothes, for example. That's not shit I usually do. Most of the women I've dated in the past expected big gestures, fancy dinners, expensive gifts, and I've gone along with the charade to avoid headaches, but I never meant any of it.

Despite our peculiar situation, I know Sunshine doesn't expect anything from me. I wish I'd followed her into the bedroom when she found all the shopping bags. I'd have loved to see the look on her face.

When I think she is done astonishing me, she reveals her tight hole is untouched, but she's more than willing to change that with me. It's crazy how that knowledge makes my heart beat so ferociously that I'm afraid it'll burst out of my chest. Never mind the crazy push and pull in my stomach.

"I'll be right back," I tell her.

Her arm shoots back as she reaches for mine. "I brought condoms. They're in one of my socks."

"You came prepared. You're such a good girl." I slap her ass.

"Ouch! Why are you punishing me if I'm a good girl?" Her brows furrow and her pout is so tempting that I almost forget about the condom.

"Punishing you?" I raise an eyebrow. "That was a reward."

"Is that a hockey player thing?"

"What do you mean?" I look for her socks.

"You know, you get hit so often doing something you love that it's altered the chemistry in your brain. Now you associate pain with pleasure."

I find a few condoms in her sock and smile. We're on the same page. I love a girl with an appetite.

"Many people find pleasure in pain."

"True. We shall see if I'm one of them." She smirks.

"I'll do my best to push your limits, beautiful. Have I ever told you I dig an adventurous lover?"

"When would you have had the time to tell me that?" she retorts, not holding back the sass.

I shake my head, then proceed to roll the condom down my shaft. "You love to talk back, don't you?"

"Only when I'm dealing with cocky hockey players."

"Is that so?" I kneel behind her and without warning, bury my cock in her pussy. She gasps loudly. "How many hockey players do you know, Sunshine?" I pull back and slam back in again, going deeper.

"Loads," she moans.

"Oh yeah? And how many have fucked you this good?"

"All of them."

Even though she's yanking my chain, jealousy makes me see red. I don't want to picture Sunshine with anyone but me.

"You're such a little liar." I move faster, spurred on by the need to possess her.

"I thought you were going to take my other virginity," she says, already breathless.

"Oh, I will, sweetheart. I need to coat my cock with your juices first."

She clenches her internal walls, increasing my pleasure. My balls tighten, and I know it's time to switch. I pull out and rub my head against her pink hole. Sunshine tenses instantly.

I lean forward, turning her face so I can kiss her hard and fast. "It's okay, gorgeous. You're in good hands."

When I ease back, her eyes are hooded. She keeps watching me while I tease her tight entrance, lathering it with her own arousal. When her hole is nice and wet, I penetrate just an inch, hissing at how good she already feels. Sunshine closes her eyes, biting her arm.

"Are you okay, beautiful?"

She nods. "I'm okay. Don't stop."

I push in another inch and stop, letting her get used to my girth. She's so tight and hot that only being inside her halfway is already making my head spin. I hold her hips, digging my fingers into her skin, and go deeper.

"You're doing so well, Sunshine." She moans in response, and when I sheathe myself all the way in, I have to pause to regain some of my control.

"I want more," she breathes out.

"You're such a filthy little slut, aren't you?"

"*Yes.*"

I begin moving my hips, slowly at first. I'm not small —on the contrary—and the fact that she's taking me without complaint is a fucking marvel. I increase my pace, testing her limits. If she tells me to stop, I will.

"You feel so fucking good, gorgeous." I press my stomach against her back as I reach for her clit. I need to use all my concentration now to not come before she does. Pleasure builds and coils at the base of my spine, giving me goose bumps.

"Oh Cody, yes."

I keep moving in and out of her while flicking her clit left and right with my finger. Our skin quickly becomes slick with sweat, and the sounds we're making are pure symphony. I move my fingers to her entrance, teasing her.

"What are you doing to me?" she murmurs.

"Keeping my promise. Do you want more?"

"Yes, give me everything."

Her words are like a shot of desire straight to my cock. I'm getting close to the edge, and I'm ready to take the leap. I insert my fingers into her pussy while I pound her ass. "Come for me, gorgeous."

"Oh my God, oh my God. I'm coming!"

And I feel it. Her body quakes, and her pussy throbs against my fingers. That snaps my self-control. I fuck her tight hole in earnest now, chasing my own release. Sunshine uses the couch to brace for my onslaught, but she doesn't know I've been holding back. I pull my fingers from her pussy to grab her hips and have better control of my thrusts.

Jesus fucking Christ. This is by far the best fuck I've ever had. A guttural sound rips from my throat as I come hard. My balls remain tight as I empty myself into the condom.

"Sunshine... fuck." I thrust one last time, and it's more a jerk than anything else.

My breathing is coming out in bursts, out of sync.

My heart is pounding violently in my chest as if trying desperately to break free. I lean forward again and plant a kiss between Sunshine's shoulder blades, making her shiver. I'm still inside her when her body slowly goes slack. I pull out, and she'd have collapsed to the floor if I didn't catch her.

"Whoa, are you okay?" I ask.

"Yes... no. I don't know."

I sit on the backs of my legs, condom still attached to my dick, and pull her onto my lap. "Did I hurt you?"

Her eyes are still foggy with lust when she replies, "Yeah, a little."

A shard of guilt pierces my chest. I lost control in the end, and I fucked her hard, forgetting it was her first time doing it like that. I'm a selfish asshole. "I'm so sorry."

"No, don't be. It was a pleasurable burn. I liked it."

I search her eyes, trying to find deceit, but she seems sincere. I kiss her softly, and when she bites my lower lip, it catches me off guard. I laugh against her mouth. "Are you trying to reciprocate, woman?"

"No. Your lips are too tempting. I couldn't resist a bite." She smiles lazily, and the oddest thing happens— my heart seems to stop beating for a second, only to take off faster than before.

I boop her nose. "You're cute when you're properly fucked."

Her brows furrow. "Are you saying I'm not cute in my normal, sane state?"

"Are you fishing for a compliment, Sunshine? You know very well you're as hot as sin, and when I'm with you, I'm walking around sporting wood like a fucking teenager."

Her beautiful eyes widen. "Really?"

"Yeah, really. Now, are you hungry?" I change the subject, not liking that I'm being so candid about the effect she has on me.

"Do you mean hungry for food, or you?" She arches a brow, making me smile.

"In this case, I mean food, but I'm hoping you *will* be hungry for me later."

"And I'm hoping this is only the appetizer, Cody. I'm not even close to being satiated."

My cock—which hasn't quite gone soft—is rock solid again. "Me neither."

sixteen

. . .

SUNSHINE

Cody is looking inside the fridge when he asks, "Do you want to eat the steak now or save that for dinner?"

"We could save it for dinner."

He looks at me. "What are you in the mood for?"

You.

The thought pops into my head unbidden, but thankfully, I don't say it out loud. He knows I want him; I don't need to mention it every five minutes. My mother always said to never let a guy know you like him better than he likes you. The key to a successful relationship is to leave the man guessing. I know her advice doesn't apply here, that there's no future beyond this cabin for Cody and me—he's a fun and yummy distraction. I'm sure it's the same for him. In a few days, we'll go our separate ways, and he'll return to his pro-hockey life filled with games and female attention.

My chest seems to grow a little bit tighter when I think about Cody with other women. It's a stupid feeling that I have no business developing. He's not mine, and he'll never be mine. Besides, catching feelings for my rebound hookup is a recipe for disaster.

"Sunshine?" Cody asks, bringing me back to the present moment.

"Yes?"

"I asked what you're in the mood to eat?"

"Oh, uh... probably something light. A salad maybe?"

He smirks. "A salad? I think we need more sustenance than that for all the cardio in our near future."

I laugh. "Fair. How about salad *and* grilled cheese?"

His brows shoot up. "How did you know grilled cheese is my favorite comfort food? Did you google me?"

I scoff. "Aren't you conceited? I didn't google you. Grilled cheese happens to be *my* favorite food."

His lips break into a wide smile. "So that's another thing we have in common."

"Oh?" I arch an eyebrow. "And what's the first?"

He moves closer, pushing me against the counter and crowding me. "How good we are in bed."

My cheeks become hot. I wasn't expecting that compliment. I never considered myself to be particularly good at sex. Adequate, yes. But it seems all I needed was the right partner to awaken the sex goddess in me.

I clear my throat. "If you want to replenish your energy, you'd better give me some room to cook."

"Right." His voice sounds raspier, and his green eyes seem to burn with lust.

He steps back, but I still feel the effect of his closeness beneath my skin like a brand that can't be removed. I hope it doesn't linger. I can't be hung up on Cody when I return to the real world. I just can't.

Cody takes a bite of my grilled cheese and moans out loud, making me laugh. "Does the sound you're making mean you like my food?"

"Like your food? That's an understatement. This is the best fucking grilled cheese I've ever had. I have half a mind to kidnap you and make you my private chef."

He's kidding, but my heart does cartwheels in my chest. Why does the idea of spending more time with Cody excite me so much?

Maybe because while I'm with him, I don't have to deal with my shitty reality.

"It's only bread, cheese, and lots of butter." I shrug.

"And your magic touch." He winks, keeping his cheeky smile in place while he takes another bite.

God, I could watch him all day. The more I stare, the more he reels me in, and not only because of his handsome face. Right now, he looks like a happy little kid having a treat.

"Aren't you going to eat?" he asks.

"Yeah. Sorry, I was daydreaming."

"I'm right here, gorgeous. You don't need to dream." His lips curl upward.

I shake my head. "Have you always been this cocky?"

He seems to ponder my question as he chews, but I can see he's pretending to think hard about it. "I've never suffered from false modesty. If that means being cocky, then the answer is yes, I've always been this way."

"Really? Even when you were a rookie in the NHL?"

"You could say I was even cockier then, I had to prove my worth."

"And how did the other players take your attitude?"

He laughs. "They gave me hell. Not my teammates though. They had my back. But rookies are always targeted by opposing teams. It's tradition. Sink or swim mentality. We need to toughen up quickly."

"It sounds brutal. I honestly don't know how you guys do it. All those hits, then traveling nonstop."

"Yes, it's intense but a lot of fun. I wouldn't trade what I do for anything else."

"That's the dream, right? Doing something you're passionate about." I take a bite of my sandwich, savoring it as well. It's one of my better ones.

"Yeah. I'm very lucky. What about you, Sunshine? What's your passion?"

I don't hesitate. "Animals. That's why I became a vet."

"That's also a profession that demands dedication."

"Yes, but like you, I wouldn't trade what I do for anything else."

He doesn't respond, but he keeps his eyes locked with mine while he chews. I hold his stare, trying to guess what he's thinking. It's an exercise in futility. I was never one to excel at reading facial expressions.

"Why are you staring at me like that?" I finally crack.

"You're staring too, Sunshine."

"Only because you are."

"I'm thinking about all the ways I'm going to fuck your tight little cunt and peach hole." Fire spreads through my cheeks. I was not expecting that answer. Cody smiles like a fiend. "I love your face. It's so... expressive."

"Shut up." I break off a piece of my grilled cheese and toss it at him. It hits his nose, then falls on his lap.

Smiling, he picks it up and eats it. "Thanks."

"Eat your food and stop making me blush," I grumble, breaking eye contact.

"Okay, boss." He stretches out his legs and touches mine under the breakfast nook table.

I try to ignore the contact, knowing Cody is determined to keep teasing me. It's an impossible task. I'm too aware of him, and I can sense his heated gaze on me. I end up inhaling my food so I can escape his scrutiny.

"Whoa, you *were* hungry." He chuckles. "And to think you only wanted a salad."

I get up from the table, taking my plate with me. "What can I say? My grilled cheese sandwiches are out of this world."

Cody's eyes soften, but the heat in his eyes seems to intensify. "Yes, they are."

seventeen

. . .

CODY

I have to get my libido in check, or I won't be able to do a damn thing besides have Sunshine flat on her back while I fuck her into oblivion. As fantastic as the idea is, I have to take it easy. I'm supposed to be resting my shoulder, after all. Using my left arm earlier to hold Sunshine in place wasn't a good idea, and my muscles are now tense and achy.

I bring my empty plate to the kitchen, and before I can get to the sink to wash it, Sunshine takes it from my hand and takes care of the task for me.

"I could have done it," I say.

"Using only one hand?"

I curl an arm around her waist and kiss her neck. "I

can do many things with only one hand and excel at them."

She melts into me, and I love the sigh that leaves her parted lips. "I know you can. But I can wash your dish, and my hands are already soapy."

"Hmm... that word gives me ideas."

She laughs. A soft sound that goes straight into my chest, making it all warm and fuzzy. What's going on with me?

"I'm not screwing you in the shower! It's too small."

"We can make it work."

"And what happens when the hot water runs out?"

"Good point." I step away from her so she can finish washing the dishes. I already have a hard-on, and the quicker she's done, the faster I can get her naked again.

I walk to the nearest window and see that it's stopped snowing. "The weather seems to be clearing."

"Oh, really?"

"If the break holds, we might be able to leave tomorrow or Monday."

"That's good." She sounds less enthusiastic, making me curious. I glance at her. Her chin is down and her attention is on the task at hand, but I notice her serious expression. I don't like that look on her at all.

"Or we could stay. We don't have to leave right away."

Her head snaps back up, and her pretty eyes are a bit rounder. "You want to stay here longer with me?"

The surprise is cute as hell, and it makes me smile. "Yeah. I'm having fun, aren't you?"

"Yes, but what if the weather turns bad again and we can't leave for another week? We'll for sure run out of food. Then what?"

"Then we walk into town, and if you freeze on the way, I promise not to eat you."

"Gee, thanks."

I walk over. "Are you done with the dishes?"

She dries her hand in the dish towel. "Yeah. Why?"

"Get naked."

Her eyebrows shoot to the heavens. "Wow, and they say romance is dead."

"Get your mind out of the gutter, woman. This time, I'm not thinking about sex," I lie. I'm always thinking about sex when it comes to her.

She crosses her arms. "Why do I need to get naked then?"

"You know there's a hot tub outside, right? It'd be a shame if we didn't use it."

And I can soak my aching muscles in scalding-hot water, but she doesn't need to know my shoulder is bothering me.

"But it's freezing outside."

"That's the whole appeal of using a hot tub during the winter." I grab her hand and tug her to me so she's flush against my body. "There are bathrobes in the closet. We'll be fine."

She scrunches her nose, becoming even cuter. "Okay. But if I catch a cold, it's on you."

"Right. Because you traipsing through the woods wearing barely anything wouldn't be the cause."

"Nope." She lifts her chin stubbornly, leaving me no choice but to kiss her.

It is meant to be a quick kiss, but it turns into a vortex of heat, engulfing me in flames instantly. I pull her closer, needing to feel every inch of her body pressed to mine. It's crazy how I can't get enough of her. She's becoming an addiction I didn't anticipate. Saying goodbye will be hard.

I ease back before I do get her naked with the intent of fucking her brains out. That's still happening in the near future, but I want to use the hot tub now that the snow has stopped.

"We'd better stop before I lose control again."

"Does that happen often?" she asks, her eyes fixated on my mouth.

"It didn't use to." I step back, not believing I told her the truth.

"Oh, and it does now?"

I narrow my eyes. "Less questions, and definitely less clothes."

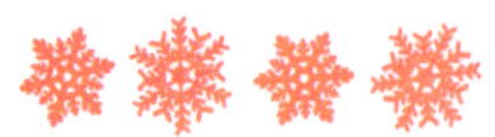

I t feels fucking divine to submerge myself in hot water. I hiss with pleasure and relax immediately. Sunshine is still hovering by the door, more inside the cabin than out.

"Come on, gorgeous. You can do it."

"It's fucking cold." She keeps her arms crossed in front of her chest.

"Not where I am. It's heaven." I tilt my head back and close my eyes.

"Oh fine," she huffs.

I open one eye and see her scurrying toward the hot tub. But she hesitates to remove her bathrobe.

"Come on, Sunshine. You can do it. I believe in you."

She sticks her tongue out. "Easy for you to say. You practically live on the ice."

"The longer you stay out of the hot tub, the colder you'll get. This is a situation where you need to shit or get off the pot."

"You're gross." She unties the robe's sash and lets it drop to her feet.

My eyes are wide open now, but she gets into the hot tub fast, and I don't get to appreciate the view for long enough.

"Oh, this feels good," she says, remaining on the other side of the tub and much too far away for my liking.

"I told you. Come here, beautiful." I stretch out my arm and take her hand.

She erases the distance between us, stopping right in front of me. Her lips are a little blue, so I run my tongue over them before coaxing them open.

Sunshine flattens her palms against my chest, tilting her head and allowing me to deepen the kiss. My cock is as hard as it can be, but I'm content to just explore her mouth for a while. I can't remember the last time I was happy just to make out with a girl. I was probably thirteen then. The moment I became sexually active, I was more interested in fucking, like any horny teenage boy.

But Sunshine is a temptress. She glides her right hand down my abs until she finds my cock.

"What are you doing, gorgeous?" I ask against her mouth.

"Nothing." She curls her fingers around my length and tugs a little.

"That doesn't feel like nothing. Are you trying to get me to fuck you in the hot tub?"

She eases back and looks into my eyes. "You can't wear protection in the tub, but that doesn't mean I can't make you come."

To make her point, she begins to jerk me off, alternating between pumping her hand up and down and caressing my head with her thumb. My balls are tightening already, and I feel like reciprocating.

I cup her pussy, using the heel of my hand to

massage her clit. Sunshine arches her back, pushing her chest toward me as if offering me her lovely breasts to feast on. I can't resist the temptation. I run my tongue over one nipple, teasing it until it becomes hard under my caress. Then I turn my attention to the other.

Sunshine increases the pace of her hand, milking my cock and making me delirious with lust. I suck her nipple into my mouth, hard, at the same time that I plunge four fingers into her pussy.

"Cody… oh my God."

I stop my caresses for a second to ask, "Do you like that, beautiful?"

"You know I do."

"You're so tight, Sunshine. It makes me wonder if you've ever been fucked properly." I press my thumb over her clit while keeping all my fingers buried deep in her.

"Obviously, I haven't." Her movements are much faster now, almost frenetic. If she keeps this up, I might come before she does.

That can't happen. It's my cardinal rule to always make my girl climax before I do.

Jesus, where did that thought come from? Sunshine isn't my girl. Lust must have fried my brain already.

I focus on my fingers sliding in and out of her heat while I flick my thumb fast over her clit. I can tell she's getting close when her hand doesn't move with the same coordination and intensity as before. I welcome the reprieve. There's nothing like being brought to the edge of an abyss and being yanked back a little. The push and pull make for a more intense orgasm.

"Cody. Yes! I'm coming." She kisses me hard before I can reply. Her entire body is shaking against mine, her pussy quivering under my ministrations.

I don't stop fucking her with my fingers until she relaxes against my body and her hand on my cock stills. My pulse is going at the speed of light, and she hasn't even made me come yet. But the moment she resumes her work, I know it won't take much longer.

"Fuck. That's it, gorgeous. You're such a good girl. Milk my cock, make me come all over your hand."

She rewards me with a sassy smile before she kisses my neck. I'm ticklish there too, but my mind is too distracted by the magic happening below to react to her devilish caress.

"Motherfucker!" I blurt out when my body convulses and I'm broken apart by the intensity of my orgasm. I wrap a lock of her hair around my fist and yank her head back to crush my lips to hers. This isn't a kiss. It's a battle of tongues and teeth.

I make Sunshine stop only when I'm completely empty and my shattered body is put back together. Breathing hard, I press my forehead against hers. "This definitely will put you on Santa's naughty list."

She chuckles. "What do you mean? You said I was such a good girl."

"Yes, but being a good girl to me means you're a naughty girl."

She pouts. "Does that mean I won't get a gift from Santa this year?"

"I don't know. Do you want a gift from that old fart, or do you want an unlimited supply of orgasms?"

She smiles. "I think I got my Christmas present early."

"I guess you did."

eighteen

. . .

SUNSHINE

Cody insisted on cooking Christmas Eve dinner, since I made the grilled cheese for lunch. It's not a fair trade, but he wouldn't let me near the kitchen. Now we're sitting at the table and eating the most amazing meal by candlelight. Besides perfectly cooked steaks, he also made the best twice-baked potatoes I've ever had in my entire life.

The fire is burning bright, and the twinkling lights on the windows contribute to making the ambience romantic and cozy. The red wine is helping too. It's easy to forget this moment won't be repeated. Most likely, if the sky remains clear during the night, we'll be able to leave the cabin tomorrow and I'll never see Cody again unless I go to a Seattle Saints game or watch him on TV. Regardless, he'll go back to being a stranger, and the thought makes me sad.

"Is there something wrong, gorgeous?" he asks.

I shake my head, hoping it will dispel the gloomy fog. "No."

"Do you wish you were with your family instead of me?" Cody smiles a little as he tries to downplay the weight of his question, but I sense a hint of wistfulness in his tone. Maybe he's having similar feelings as me.

"If you'd asked me yesterday, my answer would have been yes. But if I hadn't insisted on spending time alone, I wouldn't have met you."

His smile broadens, and a new glint shines in his eyes. "I'm glad I decided to be a Grinch and hide in the woods too."

I pick up my glass and swirl the wine. "I just realized something."

"What?" He looks at me with warm openness. It's such a contrast to the man I met yesterday.

"We fucked six ways from Sunday, and I let you fill all my holes, but I know nothing about you besides that you play for the Saints. I don't even know what position you play."

"True." He leans back, relaxing against the chair. "What do you want to know? I play defense, by the way."

"Hmm… that tracks."

He chuckles. "Why is that?"

"With your temper, it makes sense you'd be on defense."

"Why? Because you think I get to hit more people?"

"Yeah."

He shakes his head but keeps smiling. "Oh boy, you don't know much about hockey, do you?"

"Not really. My father is the obsessed fan. He wouldn't believe me if I told him I spent the weekend with you."

Cody lifts a brow. "Wouldn't? Does that mean you won't tell him?"

"Hell no. As much as he's a die-hard Saints fan, he wouldn't appreciate his daughter being defiled by one of the players." I smirk.

Cody throws his head back and laughs from the belly up.

It's such a rich sound that it awakens the butterflies in my stomach. "Oh my God. You *are* capable of feeling joy."

"Of course I am. Have I not proven that to you over and over and over again?" His eyes dance with mirth.

"That's different." I take a sip of my wine. "Let's play a game—two truths and a lie."

"All right. Do you want to start?"

"Okay." I square my shoulders. "Let's see. I've memorized the one-liners from all seasons of *Buffy, the*

Vampire Slayer. I lived in Australia for a year. And I've been arrested once."

"Hmm." He rubs his chin. "My sister is a die-hard *Buffy* fan too, so I believe it's totally possible that the first statement is true. You seem super close to your family, so I don't think you'd live a year in Australia. That's the lie."

"What?" I shriek, exaggerating my fake indignance. "You believe I've been arrested? What for?"

He bobs his head up and down. "Yeah, totally possible. As for the reason... maybe you argued with a cop that pulled you over."

"Oh my God. I'd never argue with a traffic cop. *That's* the lie!" I laugh.

His brows arch. "You lived in Australia? For real?"

"Yes. In my junior year of high school. It was part of an exchange program. The best experience of my life."

"That's pretty cool. I've been to Australia a few times. Beautiful country."

"Yeah. I loved it there. Everyone was so friendly, and the boys were cuuute."

His eyes squint. "Are you trying to make me jealous, Sunshine?"

I press my hand against my chest. "Me? Never. Besides, I didn't peg you as the type of guy who suffers from retroactive jealousy."

"I'm not that guy," he grumbles.

Okay, Cody. I'll pretend I believe you. It's silly how

giddy I become, knowing he's jealous. I can't let that go to my head though.

"If you say so. It's your turn now." I take a bite of my steak.

"Okay. I cried watching *Raya and the Last Dragon*. I was cast as Romeo in a school play. And I once worked as Santa's helper when I was in high school."

I choke on the food and suffer a coughing fit.

"Are you all right?" Cody asks.

I hit my chest with a fist. "Yep. Food went down the wrong pipe."

"Drink some wine," Cody tells me with the hint of a smile playing on his lips.

I take several sips before I dare speak again. "*Raya and the Last Dragon* is awesome and a total tearjerker. I think that's true. But the other two…" I narrow my eyes and study him. Cody keeps his expression neutral, giving me no clue. "I guess I can see you playing Romeo."

"Is that your final answer?"

"Yes."

"Nah, you're wrong. I'd never play that idiotic boy even if my life depended on it."

My eyes widen. "Are you saying you were a Santa's helper once?"

"Yep. Now you know my shameful past."

"But… you hate Christmas. Wait. Is that why?"

A shadow crosses his eyes. "No, that's not why."

"It has to do with your folks, doesn't it?"

He drinks his wine in large gulps, emptying the glass.

"You don't need to tell me. I didn't mean to pry," I continue.

He shrugs with one shoulder. "You already know I was an elf in my previous life. I might as well tell you the rest. My father knocked up my mother fresh out of high school. They made the dumb decision to get married because having a baby is a solid reason to tie the knot." His voice drips with sarcasm. "Then, to prove they didn't make a mistake, they decided to have another kid—me."

He pauses and refills our glasses. "My parents didn't make a lot of money, so it was always tense during the holidays. One year was particularly bad. My father had just lost his job, and he started drinking heavily. We didn't have money to buy a Christmas tree, so my sister and I decided to go into the woods and find a tree ourselves." Cody's eyes become unfocused as if he's reliving the story.

"To cut the story short, we got lost, and Gigi ended up with a broken arm. Instead of being filled with gratitude that we were found alive, we were yelled at, and I received an ass whooping from my father. Gigi was spared that punishment on account of her broken arm. That happened on Christmas Eve."

There's a lump the size of Texas in my throat now, and tears are forming in my eyes. "How old were you?"

He blinks fast and seems to return to the present. "I was seven and Gigi was nine. Suffice to say, we both learned that year that Santa Claus was a hoax."

"I'm so sorry that happened to you, Cody."

"It was a long time ago, but now you know." He takes another large sip of the wine.

He's trying to downplay the effect of what happened to him, but I can see how much pain it still causes him.

"I thought that catching my fiancé cheating on me with one of my friends before the wedding and only a couple days from Christmas might ruin the holiday for me."

Cody frowns. "He's an asshole. Don't let him do that to you."

I shake my head. "I won't. I can barely feel the sting of his betrayal now. Maybe it'll hurt more when I go back home. We lived together."

Cody takes a deep breath, then asks. "How long were you together?"

"Since college." I laugh without humor. "Monica—that's the bridesmaid he was screwing—introduced us. I don't know if they've been together since college, laughing behind my back, or if it's newer."

"Does it matter?"

"It does. If it's recent, then I can give myself some

slack for not suspecting anything. If it's been going on for years, then I'm a fucking dumbass."

"You're not a dumbass." He reaches across the table and covers my hand with his. "You're a beautiful, intelligent, sassy woman who turned this weekend around for me."

My eyes fill with tears again. "Stop it. You'll make me cry."

He pulls his hand back. "No, we can't have that. You can only cry after I make you come at least five times in a row, and those tears had better be of ecstasy."

"Five times, huh? Aren't you being a little optimistic." I smirk.

He returns my smirk. "Realistic, gorgeous. You'll see."

nineteen

. . .

SUNSHINE

It's Christmas morning, but I don't want to open my eyes. I'm nice and cozy under the blankets, and Cody's pressed against me. My body is tender in several places, especially between my legs. Cody made good on his promise, and the five orgasms were achieved easily, plus more after that.

His hand caresses my stomach, then it moves lower until he's cupping my pussy. I let out a moan and try to face him but discover I can't. My eyes fly open, and I find out why I can't move my arms. My wrists are tied to the headboard with the Christmas lights that were hanging over the window, and they're on.

"Cody! What did you do?"

"Merry Christmas, Sunshine." He rolls over me and rests his chin between my breasts, smiling like a fiend.

"Why am I tied up?"

"Because I've been such a good boy, and you're my Christmas gift." He runs his tongue down my stomach, leaving a trail of goose bumps over my skin.

I part my legs automatically, and my clit is already throbbing in anticipation.

"That's it, beautiful. Open them wide for me." He licks me slowly, taking his time. He's already an expert on my body, thanks to the intensive training we've had in the past thirty-six hours. He knows exactly where to lick, suck, and touch, and I want to believe it's the same for me with him.

"Cody…" Forgetting for a second that my arms are bound, I try to reach him.

"Yes, gorgeous?"

"I want to touch you."

"Not yet." He continues his merciless assault on my sensitive spot, sending ripples of pleasure throughout my body. I close my eyes, surrendering to the fact that I won't escape until he lets me.

He penetrates me with his fingers, curling them inside me. My hips buck. "Fuck!"

"Soon." He pulls his fingers from my pussy, and says, "Eyes on me, Sunshine."

I look at him and gasp when I see what he's holding now. It's one of the cone-shaped light bulbs from the

Christmas decorations, still attached to the cord. It's twinkling, like the others around my wrists. Cody's lips are curled into what I can only describe as a Grinch smile.

"What are you planning, Cody?" I ask.

"I've always enjoyed using toys in the bedroom. Since we don't have any, I thought we'd improvise."

"You aren't seriously thin—"

Cody pushes the light bulb inside me, and I have my answer. It's strange at first but not unpleasant. I'm still tense though, and my breathing becomes shallow.

"Don't worry, gorgeous. I won't hurt you." He's gentle, and I begin to relax. "How does it feel?"

"Hmm... it's beginning to feel good."

"Look at you, all lit up for me." He returns his mouth to my clit while fucking me with the Christmas light.

The strangeness of having a foreign object inside my pussy soon gives way to a sensual tingling. I get light-headed, and the room begins to spin. I don't close my eyes though, because Cody eating my pussy is so fucking hot that I could come just from watching him.

The pleasurable sensation keeps growing over my clit and inside my pussy. I bite my lower lip, a feeble attempt to focus on not climaxing too soon.

"Cody... you're killing me," I whisper.

"Do you want me to stop?"

"*No.* Don't you dare."

"You look so lush, beautiful, I can't take it anymore." He leans back, taking his delicious mouth and makeshift sex toy with him.

"Where are you going?"

"I need to be inside you, Sunshine. Right now." He rolls a condom down his erection and, using both hands, lifts my hips off the mattress.

"Cody… your shoulder."

"I don't care." He enters me with a precise and hard push, making my toes curl.

Thanks to being teased to the brink of an orgasm, being taken by him like this is enough to send me over the edge. "Oh my fucking God. I'm coming!"

Cody starts to move with intensity, sending my orgasm to new heights. The headboard bangs against the wall, and my wrists move along with it. Thankfully, he didn't tie them too tight, allowing me to turn them. So I can at least wrap my fingers around the metal bars. Cody is thrusting his hips so fast that his face is turning red from the physical exertion, and a sheen of sweat covers his forehead.

His face twists almost in agony, and I fear his shoulder is the cause, but he groans loudly in the next second, and his cock pulsates inside me.

"Sunshine… you're the fucking best." He lowers my hips back to the mattress and leans forward to slant his mouth over mine. His tongue matches the intensity of his thrusts as he takes possession of my lips.

Strands of desire twist around the base of my spine, and I come once again, but this time, Cody swallows my moans of ecstasy.

After a moment, he slows, then stops moving altogether and hides his face in the crook of my neck.

"Wow. Merry Christmas to us indeed," I say.

He leans back and looks into my eyes. "The snow has melted enough. We could leave today."

"Oh." I can't hide my disappointment, so I force some pep to my voice. "That's great news." Cody stares in silence as if trying to read my mind. "What?"

"It doesn't have to be the end."

"What do you mean?"

"I want to keep seeing you in Seattle."

My heart does several backflips and finishes with a somersault. "You want to date me?"

"Date you, fuck you.... whatever you want to call it."

As much as the butterflies in my stomach seem to be on board with the idea of keeping Cody in my life, I'm not sure if that's wise. It was one thing to forget the real world while we were snowed in. But once I return home, my problems will be waiting for me. Pro hockey players travel a lot, and they have a reputation for sleeping around. Even if I try to keep things with Cody casual, I don't want to think about him being with other women. My heart is still in pieces from Chad's betrayal.

"You don't need to answer right now," he continues.

I hold his gaze. "Okay. Now... can you untie me, please?"

He smiles. "Hmmm.... I don't know. Can I?"

"Cody!"

"Just messing with you, Sunshine."

cody

While Sunshine is in the shower, I take care of breakfast while listening to Christmas songs. I've never been domestic, and the notion that I am now brings a smile to my lips. Not getting a yes right away about my proposal hurt a little, but I'm not too worried. I know I'm not imagining things about what's going on here. This was by far one of the best weekends I've ever had, and the fact it happened during Christmas isn't lost on me. Who knew a feisty, runaway bride would make me enjoy this holiday? I now regret not getting a Christmas gift for her when I went shopping, and if my shoulder was one-hundred-percent healed, I would have gotten her a tree from the woods.

It's a miracle I haven't worsened my injury by using my left arm too much when it should stay in a sling. But I feel barely any pain now. Maybe Sunshine was good for it too.

I'm about to start cooking the eggs when my phone pings with an income message. It's Gigi, wishing me a Merry Christmas. The message was sent an hour ago, and it just got through. Service must be restored. I already checked outside and confirmed that the road is drivable. I wish I could stay holed up in this cabin with Sunshine longer, but I'm expected back in the city for my checkup.

If I reply to Gigi now, she'll call me. I'd better finish cooking breakfast first. I grab the bowl with the egg mix and add salt, pepper, and garlic powder. In hindsight, maybe I should have skipped the garlic. But if Sunshine and I both have garlic breath when we kiss, it won't be too terrible.

Kelly Clarkson's version of "Rockin' Around the Christmas Tree" is playing now, and I turn up the volume. I've never made it a secret that Kelly is one of my favorite singers.

A knock on the front door has me freezing on the spot. Who the hell is out there? For a second, I suspect Sunshine's fiancé managed to track her down. The likelihood of that happening is slim, but I get irrationally angry nonetheless.

I turn off the music and stride to the front door, body tense and ready for a fight. But when I fling the door open, I don't find Sunshine's past standing outside. I find mine.

"Penelope?"

"Surprise! Merry Christmas, my love." She leans in to give me a kiss, but I recover from my shock fast and step back.

"What are you doing here?"

"I couldn't bear the thought of you spending Christmas alone, so I came up as soon as the road opened." She lifts a basket filled with festive goodies. "Aren't you going to let me in? It's cold outside, baby."

"Cody, who's at the door?" Sunshine asks from behind me, and I curse all the fucking gods.

Penelope's eyes bug out, then burn with ire. She shoves me to the side and barges in. Under normal circumstances, I would have blocked her, but I'm too busy worrying about Sunshine's reaction to my ex.

"Who the fuck are you?" Penelope asks.

Sunshine looks at me with a myriad of questions in her eyes. Penelope is definitely crazier than I thought, and the fact that Sunshine is wearing nothing but my sweatshirt and socks screams that she's more than a stranger I got snowed in with.

"Who is this?" Sunshine asks me.

"I'm Cody's girlfriend, bitch."

"What?" Sunshine's eyes turn as round as saucers.

"She's *not* my girlfriend." I get between her and Penelope. "We've been broken up for months."

"You're such a dirty liar! If I'm not your girlfriend, how did I know where to find you?"

I turn to Penelope, angrier than I've ever been in my

entire life, and that's saying something. "I have no fucking idea how you found me. But it's clear that you're a psycho."

While I'm facing off with Penelope, Sunshine dashes past us and out the door. I try to go after her, but Penelope grabs my arm and digs her talon-like nails into my skin. "Where do you think you're going?"

I yank my arm free and glare at her. "Do not touch me. I don't know how many times I have to tell you. It's over!"

Her brown eyes fill with tears—crocodile tears. "I can't believe you're doing this to me. I love you."

The sound of a car engine tells me I've wasted too much time with Penelope. I grab my car keys and phone from the kitchen counter and run after Sunshine. She's already driving away from the cabin. Once again, she's running away, wearing barely any clothes. This time, it's all my fault.

twenty

. . .

SUNSHINE

I can't *believe* I was so stupid. Of course a guy who looks like Cody would have a girlfriend. He denied it, but what sort of crazy person would come all the way to a cabin to surprise an ex? The sting of betrayal burns more fiercely than when I caught Chad with Monica. Maybe because I let my guard down so completely with Cody, and he saw a side of me no one ever has.

I wipe away the tears that are rolling down my cheeks and try to calm down. There's still a lot of snow on the road, and the last thing I need is to get into a car accident. I can't believe I ran away wearing barely any clothes *again*. I have Cody's sweatshirt on, and I'm wearing only one sock. I had to remove the other one so I could drive without fear that my foot would slide off the pedal. I'm definitely in a way worse situation today than I was when I ran away from my own wedding, but at least I had my phone in my hand just now when I realized who'd come to the cabin.

I check the rearview mirror, half hoping that Cody is following me. When I see nothing but an empty road behind me, my heart sinks. He didn't come after me. Why would he? He's probably busy dealing with his girlfriend.

Maybe he's telling the truth, and they aren't together anymore. Now that I have time to think, and my head isn't clouded by humiliation, I believe it's possible that the woman is an unhinged ex. Unless my bullshit radar is completely busted and Cody fooled me.

I let out a shuddering breath. It doesn't matter. If anything, the drama back at the cabin is a sign that I shouldn't see Cody again or date anyone else, for that matter. Two days ago, I was supposed to get married. I can't just jump into another relationship. I need time to pick up the pieces on my own.

But understanding the right thing to do and doing it are not the same thing. My chest feels so tight I can barely breathe. And the saddest part is that I already miss Cody.

Once I leave the rural area and approach the city, I have a decision to make. If I show up at my parents' house like this, they'll have a heart attack. I don't want to ruin their Christmas morning.

I call my cousin Phyllis instead. She's the only member of my family who won't tell my parents if I show up wearing almost nothing.

"Sunshine, oh my God. I'm so glad you called. Where are you?"

"It's a long story. I'm not ready to see my folks yet. Can I stop by your apartment?"

"Yes, of course. It's only me and Crazy Tom."

Perfect. Phyllis isn't a social butterfly, and she always needs a day to recover from family gatherings. Crazy Tom is her cat, named after Tom Cruise in his jumping-up-and-down-on-Oprah's-couch era.

"Is there any chance I can park in your garage?"

Phyllis is twenty-six, the same age as me, and by far the most successful of all the "kids." Well, maybe successful isn't the right word—she's the richest, thanks to her filthy-rich clients. She's a kick-ass real estate agent and makes a lot of money selling multimillion-dollar properties. Her apartment downtown is a dream, but as far as I know, she has only one garage spot.

"Is it because you're driving the getaway car?" she asks.

"In part. You'll understand when you see me."

"Oh... Sunshine. Are you still wearing your wedding dress?" There's pity in her tone, and even though I hate it, it's better than her saying I told you so.

"No. I'll explain everything in person."

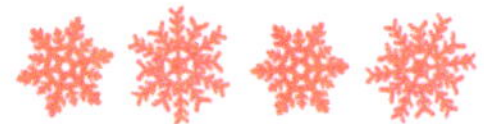

I called Phyllis when I was a minute away from her apartment and asked her to meet me in the garage and bring me a coat and a pair of shoes. She's not there when I arrive, and while I wait for her, my mind returns to the cabin and the wonderful moments I spent with Cody. Why am I more upset that he might have been cheating on his girlfriend with me than I am with Chad for actually cheating on me?

"God, I'm such a mess."

A knock on my window scares the crap out of me. I jump in my seat, pressing my hand against my chest. Phyllis is standing outside with a coat draped over her arm. I open the door and get out of the car. Her reaction is immediate.

"What the hell happened to you?" She hands me the coat.

"I'll tell you upstairs." I put the coat on fast, glad for the fuzzy warmth that follows. Then I put on the pair of Ugg boots.

In true fashion, Phyllis doesn't ask any questions during the elevator ride, but once we're in her apartment, the reprieve is over.

"Okay, you better tell me *right now* why you're wearing a guy's sweatshirt and no shoes."

"I booked a cabin in the woods at the last minute. I wanted to spend some time alone to think. But it was double-booked, and I ended up having to share it with a Seattle Saints hockey player."

Phyllis's hazel eyes bug out. "You're joking. Which one?"

"Cody Fairchild."

Phyllis drops on her white leather couch like a sack of potatoes. "You spent the weekend with *Cody*?"

I don't like how she calls him by his first name, like they're old friends. It's ridiculous to feel this way, though.

"Yes."

"What did you guys do?"

"Well..."

Her mouth makes a perfect *O*. "You hooked up!"

"Shh... you don't need to shout."

"Oh my *God*. I can't believe you hooked up with Cody. That's huge!"

"No, it isn't. Besides, this isn't a fairy-tale romance or even a very spicy Hallmark movie. His girlfriend showed up this morning."

Phyllis's brows furrow. "What girlfriend? Cody has been single for months after he ditched that blonde psycho he was dating."

I blink at her. "How do you know so much about Cody's personal life? Is he one of your clients?"

Her eyes shine with amusement. She opens her mouth to reply, but someone rings her doorbell. "Hold that thought."

She walks to the front door, and I go to the panoramic window to look at the view. The sky isn't clear, it'll probably snow again today.

"Hello neighbor," Phyllis greets whoever is at the door. "We were just talking about you!"

Uh... what?

I turn with my heart already stuck in my throat and find Cody standing in my cousin's entryway.

twenty-one

. . .

CODY

By the time I convinced Penelope to go home so I could leave the cabin, Sunshine was long gone. On my way to my apartment, I called Gigi, hoping she had Sunshine's address. After speaking with the kids for a bit, I told her about my weekend with Sunshine. At first, she gave me a tongue-lashing for seducing her guest. Then she delivered the bad news that she didn't have Sunshine's address.

I spend the rest of the drive home thinking of ways I could find out where Sunshine lives or works. I know her last name, which is something. I'm feeling hopeful when I enter my building's garage, but when I see Sunshine's car, I think I'm hallucinating. I blink a couple times, but the damn sedan with the words *Just Married* painted on the back window remains there, parked in Phyllis's spot.

There's no *way* Sunshine knows where I live. My address isn't listed. Besides, why would she come here if she was trying to run away from me?

Then it dawns on me. Phyllis's last name is Winters too. Could they be related? That's the only plausible explanation.

It's crazy how hard my heart is thumping inside my chest during the elevator ride. I've never felt this connected to someone I just met. It's not only the physical attraction that's doing my head in—believing I might never see Sunshine again was making me physically ill. Maybe I'm a glutton for punishment, or this is karma. The guy who isn't interested in commitment ends up falling for a woman who probably only wanted a weekend of fun. I was Sunshine's rebound guy, and that rarely leads to something more.

Standing in front of Phyllis's door, I rub my face. I have no fucking clue what I'm going to tell Sunshine if she's in there.

Stop being a fucking idiot and ring the doorbell already.

Phyllis opens the door. I always thought she was a knockout, with her auburn-colored hair, freckles, and killer body. But within minutes of meeting her, I knew she'd never be more than a neighbor. There's no electrifying spark between us, and I'm a firm believer in *don't shit where you eat.*

"Hello neighbor." Phyllis smiles. "We were just talking about you!"

She steps aside, allowing me to see Sunshine standing by the window. She's wearing a coat and boots now, but her legs remain bare. I can't find my voice, so I just stare at her.

"Come in, Cody."

"Thanks." I enter the apartment but don't go farther than a few steps.

"I'll be in my bedroom if anyone needs anything." She disappears down the hallway to my left, and only when I hear a door close do I dare speak.

"I can't believe you know Phyllis."

"We're cousins."

"Sunshine..."

"I know the truth, Cody. Phyllis told me you broke up with that woman some time ago. I'm sorry I over-reacted."

Worry releases its vise hold around my heart, and I can breathe more easily. I shorten the distance between us and cup her cheek. She releases a shuddering breath but holds my stare. "I understand why you left. I'd have followed you right away, but..."

"But you had to take care of your past."

"Yeah."

"And I still have to deal with mine."

"I know." My chest tightens. Is this when Sunshine tells me we shouldn't see each other anymore? Before she can shut me down, I continue. "I can wait."

Her eyes turn round. "Do you really mean that?"

"I do, beautiful. You're worth it." Tears gather in her eyes, making me wonder if anyone has ever told her that. I run my thumb over her lips, and she parts them. "I've never felt so unraveled by anyone before. This is all new to me."

"It's the same for me, which makes it all that much more confusing. I thought Chad was the love of my life, but I was more hurt believing you had tricked me than when I caught him with someone else."

I release a sigh of relief, and my heart, free from all the anxiety, speeds up to a hundred beats per minute. "I'm sorry you got hurt."

Unable to resist any longer, I lean down and kiss her softly, not knowing yet where we stand, but when Sunshine moans and opens her mouth to mine, I have my answer. I slide my hand to the back of her head and deepen the kiss, needing to breathe her in. My arm is still in its sling, preventing me from melding my body into hers. But it's safer this way. Bending Sunshine over Phyllis's couch won't do. I step back before I go supernova, but I keep touching her.

"If you want space, I can give it to you. We can take things slow."

"I appreciate that. I have to do a lot of unpleasant

things. Moving out of the apartment I share with Chad is the most pressing one."

Without a doubt, I don't want Sunshine to spend more time with her ex than necessary. Yes, I'm jealous of the motherfucker.

I keep that to myself though. "If you need help with anything, you can ask me."

She shakes her head. "Thanks, but this I have to do myself."

Satisfaction swells in my chest. There's nothing sexier than an independent woman. I run my fingers down her neck as my gaze drops to her lips. "I know I said we can take things slow, but... would you like a tour of my apartment?"

"A tour, huh?" She smirks.

I look into her eyes again. "Yeah, my place is cooler than Phyllis's."

"I bet it is. It has you in it."

Damn it. A girl after my own heart. I can't wait to see where our story goes.

epilogue

. . . .

Cody had a home game tonight, and they won. My throat is hoarse from screaming so loudly. I brought Mom and Dad to the game, and they've lost their voices too. Mom, who never cared about hockey either, became a fan once I started dating Cody.

We said we'd take things slowly, but the moment I detangled my life from Chad's, Cody and I went from slow to supersonic. He'd have had me moving in with him after a month, but I was adamant I wanted my own space for a while. The reality, I was afraid to ruin something wonderful by rushing in.

With the game over, we return to the team's private area to wait for Cody, but the first player out of the dressing room is Nate Fairchild, Cody's cousin, who also plays defense. When I first met him, I thought I was seeing double. They look so alike they could pass for twins. Their resemblance makes sense though. Cody's father and Nate's father *are* identical twins, and they both look like their dads.

"Hello, Sunshine. Good to see you again." He smiles, and as usual, his eyes shine as if he knows a secret joke that no one else is privy to.

"Hi, Nate. Good game." We hug briefly, then Nate turns his attention to my folks.

I stop listening, because Cody just came out of the dressing room, and I only have eyes for him. He's wearing a tailored dark-gray coat over his suit and wool hat. He's also clean-shaven, and that surprises me. He had scruff during the game. I run to him, and he picks me up in his arms and kisses me soundly in front of everyone. We aren't shy about our PDA.

Nate clears his throat. "Get a room."

Cody sets me down and looks over my shoulder. "Don't be a hater."

I turn in time to see Nate roll his eyes. My parents are pretending to be *very* interested in their phones.

"What are you up to this evening?" Nate asks, surprising me.

"I thought we were all going out to dinner. Did you forget?" I ask.

"Oh." He glances at Cody, and a strange gleam of guilt shines in his eyes. "Yeah, I did and made plans. Sorry about that, Sunshine."

"No worries. Another time."

"Yeah. For sure." He looks at my parents. "It was nice seeing you again. Merry Christmas."

"Merry Christmas, son," Dad replies.

"And don't forget, you're more than welcome at our Christmas Day extravaganza. The more, the merrier," Mom adds.

"Thank you. I'll try to make it." He turns to Cody and winks.

Huh? What was that all about?

Cody presses his palm against my lower back. "Ready to go?"

"Yeah."

"We'll meet you at the restaurant, son." Dad beams in a strange way.

There's definitely something going on. I wonder if everyone is acting weird because today is the anniversary of my fiasco of a wedding day. They shouldn't be. Catching Chad with Monica was the second-best thing to have happened in my life. Meeting Cody was the first. The asshole ended up moving to Miami to be with that lying bitch, so in the end, we all got what we deserved. Now I have Cody, and I couldn't be happier.

He links his hand with mine and smiles at me. My heart does several backflips, and the fluttering in my stomach is impossible to ignore. God, I have it bad for this man.

"I love you," I say.

"I love you too, gorgeous."

cody

Sunshine thinks we're going to her favorite restaurant in town, but I'm taking her to a special place. Her parents obviously know we aren't going to meet them there. They're aware of my plan. So is Nate, and the idiot almost gave it away. I shouldn't have told him, knowing he couldn't keep a secret to save his life.

Sunshine only notices we aren't going to the restaurant when I take the exit to get out of the city. She turns to me. "Where are we going?"

"Just a quick detour. I need to get something."

"Get something where?"

"You'll see."

"Cody... what are you planning?"

I quickly peel my eyes off the road to look at her. "Me? I'm not planning anything."

She narrows her eyes. "I don't buy it. Nate was acting pretty sus."

"Sus?" I laugh. "Never heard you use that term before."

"Well, it fits Nate since he's such a child."

"That's true." I focus on the road again and I can't keep the smile off my face.

"But seriously. Where are we going?"

"I'll give you one chance to guess."

It takes her a second. "Wait. Are we going back to the cabin?"

Warmth spreads through my chest. "I knew you'd guess. You're such a smart girl."

"Oh Cody. That's so romantic. But what about my parents?" Sunshine sounds guilty, and I don't want her to stress for a second.

"Don't worry. They know."

"But we are coming back for Christmas Eve, right?"

"If we don't get snowed in," I tease, smiling from ear to ear.

"Don't even joke about that."

"What? You didn't like getting stuck with me for a few days?"

She reaches for my thigh and squeezes. "You know I loved it, but I don't want to miss my parents' party again."

"If you move your hand a little bit higher, I promise we'll drive back tomorrow morning."

She hits my arm. "Stop using sex as a bargaining chip."

"Ouch, woman. I'm sore from that illegal check from Alex Kaminski."

She snorts. "The ref didn't call that one. It didn't look that hard from where I stood."

I turn to mock glare at her. "If you weren't so darn cute, I'd show you."

"Ohhh... are we having spanking tonight?"

My cock, which was already getting hard thanks to Sunshine's hand on my leg, is straining against my pants now.

"Yes, Sunshine. You can count on it."

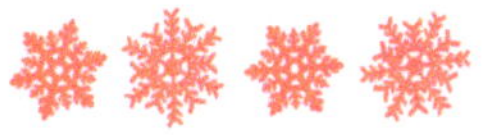

Even though it didn't snow tonight, the cabin looks like a winter wonderland, and this time, twinkling lights hang from the wraparound porch.

"Cody... did you do this?"

"Do what?" I pretend I don't know what she's talking about. I came here a couple days ago to set everything up. The outdoor lights are on a timer. I also made sure Gigi didn't double-book the cabin again. She met Sunshine when we visited the family in San Diego after my niece was born. They became instant friends.

"The cabin looks so pretty."

I park the truck and say, "I didn't want to arrive here and feel like we were entering the set of a horror movie."

"Yeah. It was pretty spooky last year."

"I can't believe you were brave enough to get out of the car," I joke.

"I was highly motivated." She opens the door and gets out of the truck.

I follow her, not wanting to miss her expression when she sees the surprise I prepared for her. She types in the code for the lock without having to look up the number.

"You memorized the password?"

She looks at me, smiling. "I wouldn't forget such a memorable number."

I touch her face with the tips of my fingers. "I didn't forget either."

She pushes the door open, and I let her walk in first. The Christmas tree lights up automatically. Motion sensor for the win.

Sunshine gasps, covering her mouth with both hands. "Oh my God, Cody. You got me a tree!"

"I would have gotten you one last year, but it would've been too hard with the use of only one arm."

She turns to me and throws her arms around my neck. "Thank you, it's beautiful." She kisses me with such passion that I almost forget about the other surprise.

Reluctantly, I pull back. "You should check under the tree. Maybe Santa brought you an early gift."

She doesn't say anything as she steps back and walks to the tree. I put her gift in an oversized box on purpose. Sunshine drops to her knees and slides the box closer to her. "What did you get me, Cody?"

I cross my arms, nervous now that the moment is upon me. What if she hates what I got her? "You'll have to open it and find out."

She destroys the wrapping paper eagerly and lifts the lid, finding only colorful packing paper inside. Then the search begins, and soon, the floor is littered with strings of paper. Her brows furrow when she finally locates the gift. She pulls the puck from the bottom of the box and turns to me. "You gave me a puck?"

"Yep."

"I don't want to sound ungrateful, but why?"

I walk over and crouch next to her. "Turn it over."

She flips the puck and gasps. The diamond ring embedded in the back of the puck glitters, reflecting all the twinkling lights on the tree. Sunshine looks into my eyes, her own shining with tears. "Cody..."

I take the diamond ring from the puck and hold it between my thumb and forefinger. "Sunshine, this past year with you has been the most wonderful, surprising, and fulfilling year of my entire existence. I was a hollow man before you came into my life. But the fire I saw in you when you threw that bottle of whiskey at me spoke to me in more ways than one. I had no idea what I was getting into, but I wanted to know more about the mysterious woman in the wedding dress."

Tears run down her cheeks, and I take that at as a good sign. I lick my lips and continue. "Even when you were in pain, you gave without asking for anything in return. You risked your life to make sure your parents knew you were okay. You gave me a chance, despite me being a grumpy asshole."

"You weren't always an asshole," she butts in.

I smile. "And you always see the best in everyone. You'll never know how much I love you, and if you agree to marry me, I'll spend the rest of my life showing you."

Her hands are shaking when she wipes the moisture from her cheeks. "Cody, I don't know what to say. This is all so thoughtful."

My stomach plummets through the earth. There's a *but* coming. I know it.

"But..."

There. I knew it. Adrenaline spikes in my veins, making my heart pump faster. And damn, my eyes are burning. But I'm not gonna cry, at least not in front of her.

Sunshine jumps to her feet and yanks a string of lights off the tree. "But before I say yes, I need to know if you're willing to get tied up and fucked by an ornamental light bulb in the name of love."

The heart that was withering jolts in my chest. I unfurl from my crouch, take her left hand, and put the ring on her finger. "Yes, my love. For you, I'll do anything, even turn into a damn firefly."

Her face splits into the brightest smile. "Then yes, Cody, I'll marry you."

THE END

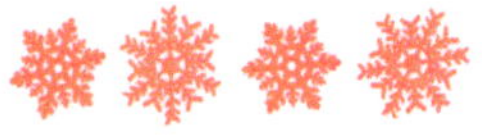

Thank you so much for reading Sunshine and Cody's story. I hope you loved it. Please consider leaving a review.

If you want more romance stories featuring swoony hockey players, I recommend my PLAYERS OF HANNAFORD U series.

Start with PLAY IT DIRTY, a fake dating, he falls first romance. **ONE-CLICK NOW!**

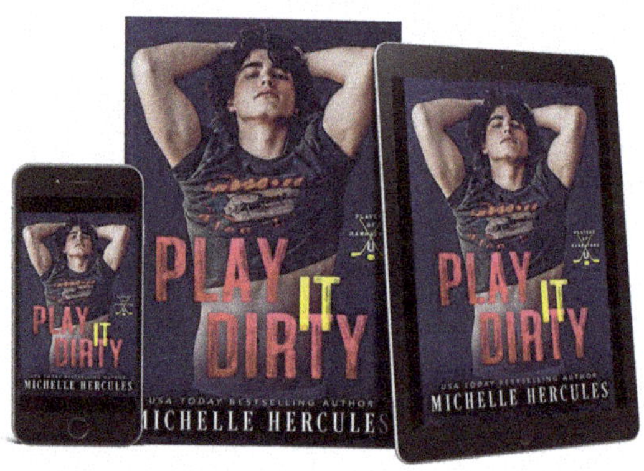

Despite my last name being Kingsley, I had to work hard for my crown. I'm a gifted hockey player but earning a spot on the Hannaford U hockey team took more than talent.

When it comes to dating, that's a different story. I've always had it easy. There's never been a girl I couldn't win over.
Until I met Gia Mancini, a goddess among mortals—not only did my charms not work on her, she friend-zoned me.

But our story isn't over yet. She messed up, and the only way she can fix her mistake is by agreeing to fake date me.
Now the game is on, and I'm not opposed to playing it dirty.

ONE-CLICK NOW

Merry
Christmas

about the author

USA Today Bestselling Author Michelle Hercules always knew creative arts were her calling but not in a million years did she think she would become an author. With a background in fashion design she thought she would follow that path. But one day, out of the blue, she had an idea for a book. One page turned into ten pages, ten pages turned into a hundred, and before she knew it, her first novel, The Prophecy of Arcadia, was born.

Michelle Hercules resides in Florida with her husband and daughter. She is currently working on the *Blueblood Vampires* series and the *Filthy Gods* series.

Sign-up for Michelle Hercules' Newsletter:
bit.ly/MichelleHerculesVIP